Flying South

No. 9

2022

Managing Editor: Steve Lindahl

Poetry Editor: Mary Hennessy

Non-Fiction Editor: Jennifer Stevenson Vincent

Fiction Editor: Ray Morrison

Fiction Readers: Bob Shar
Steve Lindahl

President's Favorite chosen by:
Judie Holcomb-Pack

Cover Art: Barbara Rizza Mellin

Flying South is a literary magazine/writing contest published annually by Winston-Salem Writers, an association of writers and readers with the purpose of:

Building community and helping writers improve their craft.

Information about Winston-Salem Writers can be found at the website: **www.wswriters.org**

Winston-Salem Writers is a non-profit organization and a partner with The Arts Council of Winston-Salem and Forsyth County, NC.

Contents

Non-Fiction:

Poetry:

Nick T. Watson

The Old Man Who Thought
He Could Become Garcia Marquez

While entertaining his dream of becoming the American Gabo, Rodrigo Buonaventura had discovered a troubling fact, he was becoming invisible.

Rodrigo was a familiar sight in the small Florida coastal town of Macadamia, the old man in a rather shabby white suit holding court in the local coffee shop trying to convince anyone within earshot that he could become the American Garcia Marquez. This extravagant assertion motivated the few townspeople who knew of the existence of Garcia Marquez to shout in fond exasperation, "That is ridiculous, Rodrigo, you're not from Colombia and you cannot write!" But he would wave their complaints away with a skinny and deeply tanned arm, his loose-fitting gold watch slipping and sliding up and down his sinewy forearm that was crisscrossed with the erratic snaking of thick blue veins. "Listen," he would say, "America has sent men to the moon, think of that! And just so they could pick up stones and hop around the lunar landscape in slow motion! America has made cars that drive themselves and helicopters that have landed on Mars. Yes, my friends, America is the land of miracles and I am an American, so think of that!"

Rodrigo had become aware of his increasing invisibility while doing his shopping in Macadamia's only supermarket, a dreary Wynn Dixie that looked as sad and beat up as an aging small town former beauty queen stumbling around on heels way too high, a skirt far too short for her pudgy thighs and her puffed up face dripping with a sadness that no amount of make-up could hide.

He could be seen almost daily, shuffling around the produce section carefully choosing his fruits and vegetables, usually a mix of tomatoes, cucumbers, apples and oranges. He took his time, checking them for the right color, the necessary firmness, the absence of flaws, blemishes, bruises and, yes, sins. The first suspicions of his invisibility came to him slowly with the realization that he could no longer find attractive women eyeing him surreptitiously with what he had always thought was fleeting but unabashed lust. He had also convinced himself that he could see the cheeky tips of their tongues moistening their lips in what could only be unconscious amatory anticipation. When becoming aware of his newfound invisibility he had shrugged his shoulders, accepting the cruel fact that he had become just another shuffling old man in the produce section. Yes, he had become invisible, but he was still going to become the American Gabo. This dream had not come to him while asleep but when sitting in his favorite deckchair by the pool. He had jumped up in excitement, startling the people nearby. "*Si!*" he had shouted,"I will become the American Garcia Marquez and those women will quiver and tremble in excitement when they set eyes on me, for not only will I become visible again, but I will do so as the Great Gabo!"

Truth was he hadn't always been an American. There was the little matter of his other life, the one he had left behind in Buenos Aires, Argentina's giant, snarling metropolis. "Yes, my friends," he would tell the coffee shop patrons, "living in Argentina is like finding yourself in a strange casino at three am, your mind ablaze and raging from the alcohol sloshing about in your skull, your money gone, an empty glass in your hand and in the din all you can hear is the croupier calling out your favorite numbers, the ones on which you would have placed tall, tottering stacks of chips. And you suddenly realize how afraid and alone you are, for you have become that most worthless of creatures, the failed, defeated gambler in a crowded casino, your pockets empty even of the few coins that might buy you another drink. This fear will grip your soul like a python squeezes the final vestiges of life from its prey. Your breathing will become labored and painful, sharp gasps that fill you with dread for you know you will end up in a curled heap on the cold casino floor even as hordes of frantic gamblers, their pockets bursting with casino chips, their hands clutching thick wads of cash step over your crumpled body without even giving it a cursory glance."

"Yes, my friends, I speak with first hand knowledge of this for I have lived through that very nightmare. I have found myself in that casino at precisely 3 am, desperation gnawing at my soul like maggots feeding on a still warm body. But something happened that night, my friends, something that would alter my life forever. For I saw a woman staring at me. She was a flaming redhead, her hair wild as an out of control prairie fire. She was skinny and very tall, her body sucked into a tight bright green mini dress. Some cartilage had been crudely sawn off her nose, her lumpy breasts were swollen with cheap Chinese silicone, her lips puffy and strained with fat transplanted from some mysterious dark fold in her buttocks. But it was her eyes and fingers that transfixed me. Her fingers were long and thin and all I could think of, even in the drunken turmoil of my mind and with death whispering in my ear, was how those fingers would feel traveling over my body discovering pleasures and emotions I had forgotten or did not know existed. And her eyes! Green, a bright shiny green like the moist Spring leaves of a young and trembling sapling, but they were also the eyes of a tiger, an angry tiger, crouched and ready to pounce, its jaws open, fangs glistening, the muscles of its flanks and thighs tensed and coiled, like steel springs ready to explode into action. As I looked at this woman I felt a distant familiar stirring in my loins and realized I was still alive, that there was hope. A fleeting one, perhaps, but I could feel the warm rush of bubbling blood in my veins and arteries, the faint clicking of brain cells coming back to life; a rush of desire so powerful it swept through the thick haze that had engulfed my mind and body. I was no longer that penniless gambler, I was now a fearless warrior, a mighty *conquistador* waving a shiny sword, leading an invisible army into battle against the most formidable of enemies. But inebriated by that rush of desire and lust I was really no more than a praying mantis, that most tragic of lovers who will search out the object of his desire knowing full well that he will mount her, fill her with his seed and then, even before the explosion of ecstasy, she will turn on him and chew his head off. And so my friends, on that fateful night I stared back at that woman, standing ram-rod stiff, yes, stiff as a young man's brash virility and shouted vile threats, screaming until my vocal chords were ripped to bloody shreds as I spewed bright red spittle in long slow arcs. My friends, what happened to me that night is what it is like to live in Argentina. It is a dangerous and sometimes beautiful life, full of deafening noise,

Nick T. Watson 3

cruel treachery and a deep unforgiving sadness. But that night changed the course of my existence. Later, as I lay beside that woman, our bodies spent, I could hear the sound of the sweat on our bodies cooling and when I leaned over and licked the cheap alcohol-drenched sweat from her armpits she turned her head, looked at me with those green eyes and whispered, "You have to go." It was at that precise moment, my friends, that I knew I was being told to leave Argentina. Those words carried the promise of some distant place waiting for me, somewhere I could be at peace and not fear the very act of being alive. A place where I could be reborn, where it might be possible to find someone with whom to share a new life. Maybe this magical twist of fate would lead me to that wondrous place and grant me the warm simplicity of a smiling girl with dimpled thighs sitting naked by my side, holding my hand and whispering tender words into my ear. And so, my friends, it came to be that I packed a bag with my stories and prepared to leave."

This leave-taking was not to be easy Rodrigo explained, "First I had to sever all bonds with the city of my birth and to achieve this I had to walk the streets of Buenos Aires on the darkest of nights, the damp air filled with the shrieking of sirens and the barking of a million invisible dogs and face the unspeakable and inevitable dangers lurking on even the friendliest looking corners. I was forced to confront deranged strangers that in their madness held terrible grudges against life itself, the stench of the poison in their blood coming off in overpowering waves, but I bombarded them with vile obscenities that came from some dark place, hissed terrible warnings at them through clenched teeth, warnings so dire and awful they loosened my sphincter and I could feel trickles of warm excrement coursing down my legs. I have stared into the eyes of madmen who held knives to my throat and pushed them away while threatening to tear the jugulars from their necks with my bare hands, gouge out their eyes with my thumbs, smash my knee into their groin to explode one testicle and banish the other to some dark body cavity they didn't even know existed. I have looked into the barrel of a gun held just inches from my face, the finger on the trigger miraculously kept in check thus sparing me. But, my friends, for all the unspeakable horrors and dangers the city vomited up at me I am now here, an American in America. Yes, I packed a bag with my stories and prepared to leave, even knowing full well that the aroma, the images and sounds, the very feel of Argentina would always remain with me."

Rodrigo would tell this story, and many others, repeating them again and again, refusing to acknowledge the blunting of their impact that came with repetition. "Yes, my friends," he would begin, "when God created Argentina he had become weary, all he had was one week to create all this, think of that, just seven days! I suspect that Argentina was one of his last creations and in his weariness he had maybe lost some of the clarity of his mission. I should not say this, *y que Dios me perdone,* but it must be true." Rodrigo would sigh, "I have driven across the arid, treeless stretches of San Luis, the mighty Andes looming in the horizon and driven past giant spiders the size of soup bowls, seen them flatten down as if prepared to jump as I roared past. Did they jump, were they clinging to the side of my car? Fear made me push down the accelerator with the hope that this would blow them off. Or were they still hanging on, grinning maniacally, secure in the knowledge that sooner or later I would have to stop? This is the fear that comes with living in Argentina, it is ever present and takes on wild, weird shapes that are impossible to confront and defeat. Our souls are swallowed up in a sea of foul bile and all we can do is whimper and try to hide, and as we lie in the fetal position in some dark corner, hoping we won't be seen, all we can do is listen to the sound of the dust settling around us, and it is a mysterious and magical sound that drowns out the desperate beatings of our heart."

Rodrigo finally left Argentina late on a Tuesday night red-eye to Miami, a nine hour non-stop flight. "It wasn't easy coming to America," he would recall, "Imagine how it must have felt. I was going to Florida. Think of the visions that flooded my mind like massive waves from a burst dam. Giant pythons wrapped like wild lovers around stoic palm trees; slow-moving alligators with unblinking eyes gliding soundlessly through the dark swamp waters, barely disturbing the surfaces. And the flamingoes! Vast, vibrant splashes of vivid pink, giant flocks of them that at some silent and secret cry of warning would take off as one, an immense pink swarm that torched the blue sky rendering it bright red, like a torrent of blood flowing from the heavens. The cries, calls and songs of a multitude of mysterious birds blending into wondrous waterfalls of music. Yes, my friends, the visions of Florida were like a magical trip to an exotic place. Thick forests of chilling, strange-shaped trees half submerged in murky swamps; multitudes of orange and grapefruit groves, like vast massed armies, stretching as far as the eye can see. And the beaches! Crowded to bursting point with shiny, near naked multitudes that spoke in every language imaginable and were ready to break free of all constraint and indulge in the crazed pursuit of pleasure, however forbidden or daunting. And the heat! Buenos Aires is a hot, sticky city that will embrace you in a choking, clammy grip, but there is not a heat like that of Florida's. You can stand still, under a palm tree, knee-deep in a thick manicured carpet of sawgrass, your body bereft even of the slightest quiver, your breathing slow and paused and yet the heat will overpower you and the sweat will pour off you in gushing torrents. Yes, my friends, Florida is a strange, magical place that suggests that everything is possible, where disaster is perhaps only a short step away but also where all dreams, however fantastic, may come true."

Rodrigo would pause here, "But, my friends, getting out of the Miami airport is the first battle, for the doors to Florida are tightly closed. Those excited planeloads of tourists, immigrants and asylum seekers will be herded into a vast hall, forming endless lines of people from the world over. This will soon be a silent crowd, any excitement they may have felt will soon evaporate for they know that their hopes and dreams are now in the hands of unsmiling officials that hold the key that could open the door to Florida, but just as easily, and with a mere dismissive wave of their hand, could banish them to a spartan little room, that dreaded first step to being sent back to their place of origin. Those subdued crowds will realize just how ephemeral are their hopes and dreams," Rodrigo would explain, "Yes, they would do well not to look too worried, or even too unconcerned, for there are people walking up and down those lines, specially trained people who with one look can detect who should be pulled out and marched away. They are like drug-sniffing dogs these inspectors, they look into your eyes and can see your soul. They can hear the nervous twisting and writhing of your frightened gut, they can hear the accelerated pumping of your heart as clearly as a drum beat in a carnival parade. They will spot the slightest nervous twitch of your fingers but above all, they can smell your fear." Rodrigo would pause, "But if you survive the line then you will come face to face with the uniformed person at the desk. Some will treat you curtly and coldly, trying to curdle your blood with fear, trip you into some tragic response that will get you pulled away. Others will be polite and friendly, too friendly, and even as they make innocent small talk with you they are prying into your soul and mind with their questions. They will take photos of your face, scan your eyes, check your finger prints and pore over your documents. So what do you do for a living in Argentina Mr. Buonaventura? You've come just in time for good weather, how long are you planning on staying and where? I see this is your first visit." Rodrigo would look at his audience, "With fear beginning to gnaw at my soul I looked into the eyes of the official and then the big surprise. He smiled at me, held out my passport and said, "*Bienvenido a Miami, señor Buonaventura.* Yes, again, magic, my friends!"

Rodrigo would smile, "Imagine, America had opened its doors! I was in America and would one day become an American. I knew this was to be my destiny. I would conquer Miami and drive around South Beach in a white convertible Rolls Royce with adoring crowds cheering my name. Yes, as I walked out of the airport, drunk with the fantastic images of my future I could see myself dancing down Calle Ocho to the sweet, voluptuous sound of salsa music, drinking mojitos, eating *arroz y frijoles negros,* my soul filled with the sweet sound of Cuban accented Spanish, my eyes wide to breaking point with the sight of the beautiful women of Little Havana and South Beach. Yes, my friends, I took my passport from that official and as I thanked him tears sprung from my eyes and flowed like mountain springs after a long winter."

A few months later Rodrigo had moved north looking for the place he knew awaited him, and he found it in Macadamia Beach. An unremarkable and drab little beach town like so many others that had spread up and down the East coast of Florida sprouting like weeds in an unkempt garden. These towns were kept in place, pressed up against the coastline by the endless and uncaring I-95 highway that sped past as if ashamed of them. To the constant traffic on the Interstate these towns all looked alike, dreary little strips malls harboring clutches of pharmacies, check-cashing offices, furniture stores, thrift shops, fast food joints, used car lots, sleazy bars, beat up grocery stores, massage parlors, banks and the inevitable cluster of shabby old motels, run-down Howard Johnson and Ramada Inns.

And so Rodrigo made his home in the beachside Playa Brava Motel of the little town of Macadamia where he would spend twenty happy years aging in synchronicity with his drab little one bedroom suite. While he lost most of his hair, muscle tone and looks the motel's suite carpets went threadbare, the stained mattress slowly sagged into deep, sad valleys and a musty smell slowly enveloped them both and made it their own.

Rodrigo shared the motel with other year-round guests who were mostly old, fat and retired. The men flopping about poolside, like obese and shiny walruses, their rolls of fat shimmying in the sun as they reached out to their ever present margaritas in tall glasses, little plastic umbrellas clipped to their rims. Most of the women were skinny, tanned deep brown and shriveled-up like vacuum-packed California raisins. They tried to hide this cruel reality behind overblown sunglasses, their lips bright red gashes in a sea of angry wrinkles, their hair stiff and brittle, held in place by clouds of hairspray, their arms cluttered with jangling jewelry. Rodrigo would look at them and smile fondly, these are my people now, we are members of the same tribe.

Another of his favorite places was the town's coffee shop, "Joe's Coffee", a small, cluttered little place whose walls still reeked of decades of now forbidden cigarette smoke. The shop's furniture and fixtures were as ancient and beaten as most of its regular year-round customers. Rodrigo, decked out in his shabby white suit and a sweat-stained Panama hat soon became a regular himself. He wore blue-tinted sunglasses, a white shirt unbuttoned half way down his chest and scuffed white tennis shoes; his body dangerously sun-tanned. He sometimes took a book to the coffee shop but invariably ended up telling and retelling his stories. Garrulous and affable by nature Rodrigo was soon accepted as one of their own by the coffee shop regulars and with them he found a family of sorts and an audience for his stories. It was also true that after the multitude of repetitions their attention would sometimes begin to waver. Some would drift back to their crosswords, or stare with blank gazes at the silent news scroll on the TV while quietly stirring their coffees, lost in mysterious thoughts that no one would ever be privy to.

Rodrigo also loved sitting by the motel's pool, it's surface shiny with sweat and sunscreen grease. It was usually empty but for a solitary old lady slowly doing a breast stroke and a couple of fat old men standing in the shallow end chomping on cigars and muttering to each other. Rodrigo wore his sparse white hair cropped short, shaved but twice a week, and there was always a patch or two that would escape the razor and these little tufts would sparkle in the sun. He had been good looking as a young man but the passage of time had left deep creases carved into his face, his eyelids drooped low over his watery blue eyes, large puffy bags hanging under them and his nose had thickened. Sometimes he'd catch his reflection in an unexpected mirror and for a second or two would not recognize himself.

"Hey, Rodrigo, tell us about the week Argentina had three Presidents."

The regulars at the coffee shop and the lodgers in the Playa Brava Motel had all heard Rodrigo's stories so often they had their favorites and would periodically request them.

"No, tell us about the night club dancer that became President!"

"Yeah, tell us a story, but a happy one, we don't need to hear about the Disappeared."

"The war with England, tell us about that!"

Rodrigo soon developed friendships with many of the coffee shop regulars and also with the young baristas. One of them had become his favorite. Tall and lanky, hair dyed bright copper, green eyes that more often than not appeared to blink back some unspoken, secret sadness. Ashley, was her name and she had a long snake tattooed down one of her arms.

They slowly developed a relationship that neither of them really understood and did not question. They confided in each other like lovers might but had wordlessly accepted that their relationship was something different. But even with these unspoken limitations to their relationship they played important roles in each others lives and Rodrigo knew that his was the lesser one. He would tell her about his life, loves and problems in Argentina, stories filled with personal details that were not present in those he made public and she would encourage him to put them in writing. "You really should, Rodrigo, you've had such an amazing life, so many incredible stories and people love hearing them." She bought him a notebook and made him promise he'd begin writing. "Just write them down, make notes that later you can edit and rewrite." And so he had started filling page after page with nervous and hurried handwriting. He would show her the notebook and Ashley would smile, "Oh, Rodrigo, I am so proud of you! This notebook will become a book everyone will talk about!" She would give him a hug and Rodrigo would hold her tight and whisper, "Ashley, maybe I am already the American Garcia Marquez and only you know it. It is our secret and if it ever gets to be known you will be recorded as my mysterious muse."

Rodrigo told her about his marriage and divorce, "It was doomed from the start, we were both fearful of commitment so we ended up living in silence, just eyeing each other with distrust, a strange anger in our souls slowly coming to a boil. We knew better than to blame each other and so finally we parted, amicably. We still wish each other happy birthdays," he added with a smile. "Yes, my life then became like a train trip with the obligatory stops at unknown stations being the women I met and loved. Today I will tell you that trip went on for too long but it is over now, I have reached the end of the tracks. Yes, all trips good or bad do come to an end but the memories live on."

Ashley would tell him about the men that slipped in and out of her life and how these relationships always ended in disappointment. "Sometimes I think there must be something wrong with me, why do they always move away? Why am I so often alone? It makes me desperate, Rodrigo, this loneliness, it clouds my judgement. Maybe I fall into these relationships too easily. "

"Oh, don't be sad, Ashley, you are special and somewhere there is a special man who is waiting to walk into your life, and when he does it will be like a massive door swinging open and happiness will pour in and embrace you. Ashley, you are a rare gem and one day the heavens will open up and shower you with a multitude of rainbows. You will be happy, that day will come, I promise you." And Rodrigo would silently implore God to banish the sadness from her eyes.

Ashley would look at him and smile, "That's so sweet Rodrigo, I hope you're right, but, let's talk about you, you must have some special lady friend." Rodrigo laughed, "Yes, it is true, I have a friend at the motel, a wonderful woman nearly my age, beautiful and wise. We share the love of our privacy and solitude and enjoy our moments of occasional intimacy. We are good, Ashley, I am a lucky man."

Usually their conversations were more playful, "Rodrigo, why do you play the Lotto, you know it is almost impossible to win." Rodrigo smiled, "Ah, my beautiful sweet Ashley, you don't understand, it is not about winning. It is about dreams and expectations. I know I will not win those millions, but I spend them! Oh yes, I travel to magical far off places, some which I didn't even know existed. I dance with beautiful, exotic women whose languages I don't understand and feast on food so rich and savory my taste buds scream in ecstasy. Yes, Ashley, I live out all my dreams and fantasies, however wondrous these may be so it is never a disappointment when my numbers don't line up." A smile so soft and tender came to Ashley's face it brought tears to Rodrigo's eyes. She reached out across the table and laid her hand on his, "Oh Rodrigo, you are a crazy man."

As the sun set each evening Rodrigo would sit by the pool and listen to the deafening screeching of a zillion frogs and he'd smile, for somehow by the time he got to bed the racket would respectfully come to a sudden end. They think of everything in America, he would smile. They have even found a way to keep dogs from barking, sending them to training schools where they are taught to refrain from that most doglike of features.

Inevitably the day that Rodrigo had always dreaded finally came to pass. Ashley asked him out to dinner and they had gone to a restaurant they both liked, one with real white tablecloths, soft lighting and the absence of live music.

"Rodrigo, I have something to tell you and it hurts and saddens me," Ashley confessed, and Rodrigo knew what was coming, "I am leaving Macadamia, Rodrigo, I am going to Los Angeles."

Rodrigo looked at her in shocked silence and felt as if life itself was draining from his body for he too had something to confess and the words he now would not utter had played out in his mind many a time. Ashley, I am an old man who has lived a long and lucky life but my body and I, inseparable friends that we have been for so long, have now become estranged. We are no longer one. My body has moved away and taken on a new identity and I do not recognize this stranger who wakes me up when night is at its darkest and most silent. He leans over me, this stranger, almost smothering me while whispering deathly threats that I know will soon come to pass. I now have a recurring dream in which I am absolutely naked and walking down a street in the pouring rain. I can see myself so clearly, Ashley, a tired old man, his body now beaten and shrunken and as I look around I can see people watching me through their windows. Some of them are smiling and waving, others are scowling and shouting words I cannot hear. When I wake I lie in bed shivering and shaking for I know this is death that beckons. But I do not fear this death march, Ashley, for you will be with me holding my hand even if I cannot see you. But Rodrigo kept quiet, his confession unspoken and they had finished their last meal together in a silence he would always regret and parted with an almost desperate embrace that even in its silence spoke like they never had.

It was the pool boy who found him. Rodrigo was sitting by the pool, his eyes were closed but his sad smile confused the boy who thought he was simply resting.

But Rodrigo had gone, taking his stories with him. The silence

he left behind took over, and in time he was forgotten, as is always
the case.

Joyce Schmid

Waiting Room for the CVOR

Cold light.
A clock. A clock.

Earlier, a nurse in full hijab,
her forehead on the chapel floor

in prayer for my loved one's heart.
أَسْأَلُ اللَّهَ الْعَظِيمَ رَبَّ الْعَرْشِ الْعَظِيمِ أَنْ يَشْفِيَكَ.

Now—in the hall--
an Aztec priest

with eagle warriors and *huehuetl* drums
advancing on the temple stairs.

O God— Jehovah—Yaweh— Holy Trinity— Allah—भगवान् –
        Huitzilopochtli—
I call on you.

Outside, the full moon slips
into the crimson shadow of the earth—

both creatures of reflected light like me—
all held in our motion by the force

that through the black hole drives the stars—
stars ripped apart (if Einstein had it right)

and squeezed into the Singularity,
then blasted white-hot out the other side,

astonished to emerge alive

as purer fire.

Notes:
1- COVOR is the cardio-vascular operating room
2. أَسْأَلُ اللَّهَ الْعَظِيمَ رَبَّ الْعَرْشِ الْعَظِيمِ أَنْ يَشْفِيَكَ—Arabic prayer: "I ask
Almighty God, Lord of the Great Throne, to heal you.
3. *huehuetl* is pronounced "weh-weht"
4. भगवान्--Bhagavān
5. Huitzilopochtli is pronounced "weet·see·luh·**poach**·tuh·lee"

Genevieve Allaire

The Guadalupe Confessionals

To swim in a pool with the sun overhead at noon, shadows cast below you effervescent, ephemeral, wriggling through your grasp as the water through your paddled fingertips. You are here and then not, flipping and bouncing off the pool wall, returning each time.

You can only live for this illumination, swimsuit lines seared into your skin as the tight embrace of a midday sky. Here and then not.

I believe in ghosts because I am one.

I have lived in New Mexico for three years, but my consciousness continues to float in the dewy piedmont of the north coast, swaying and receding with the rolling hills, fluttering behind clouds. I soar through meadows, circling the places where I lived or died, again, and again, and again.

And it is as true as the rest of it: That I am still alive, here in the southernmost point of New Mexico. I live and breathe, in and out, my pupils the size of the sky. If you listen closely, you can hear a whistle and a rattle, the wind come to take us all.

Here and then not.

One ghost floats around the vacant shelter in Carlsbad, New Mexico. I oscillate between amorphous clouds hanging low in the oil town, east to west. The vibration of hail plummeting into sudden streams stiffens me frozen in fear. I slash dewy clouds piecemeal in search of the sun, but once again, the light has eluded us all.

The waters rise.

I see that the roads have become the sky, one reflection, merged in the union of saturation. Too soon the floodwaters surge and swallow a truck whole. To the north, the waters would claim another vehicle, this time with a woman inside of it.

I want to impart greater wisdom than I am able. I see that the floods and the drowning which escaped me were the impetus I needed to leave.

I have lived many places, but I have died in even more.

In each of these places, a ghost of myself resides. The natural outcome of a life defined by loss is the accumulation of hauntings I abscond to when I feel as if the vast expanse before me might swallow me whole.

***

My parents, my brother, and I lived in the forest, once, back in New Jersey, where the thick humidity led to a proliferation of plants that threatened to smother buildings, roads, and human civilization itself. Here in the New Mexico desert, plants cannot proliferate, because they have a more important duty: Adapt to the unforgiving conditions, or die. The resurrection plant, which needs no root system, can curl up and sweep across desert plains, pushed by winds, until it reaches water, where it will unfurl and reproduce in splendor. Honey mesquite, with a taproot up to 33 feet deep, plunges into the depths of caliche and sand in the ultimate pursuit for water and, therefore, sustenance.

All of these plants have one thing in common: They survive.

***

Ghosts of memories believe they are worthy company.

Should you choose to ignore Memory's knock, your life will becoming a waking horror. You will live a life of fright, cowering at the top of the stairs, unable to escape from Memory's threats, the frantic banging causing the door to thud in its frame, cracking drywall at the insistence of Memory's right to enter. You will remain crouched in cowardice, rendered static in panic. Time will become your abstract warden, taunting you and denying you the length of your sentence. You will spend your potentially infinite condemnation staring at a stuck clock wrapped in ivy, crossing over itself without pause.

And when Memory inevitably crosses the threshold into your current home, you will be punished for denying it so long. There is no forgiveness for "eventually". You waited, and now you will suffer.

Memory leaves a trail of lavender Fabuloso in the air and dusty echoes in your mouth as she tears your drywall ceiling to floor, screaming as only the denied can. Amidst these screams, you can decipher a song, one of threats, of darkness, and of remembering.

You weren't always alone, after all. You had your brother, and your mother, and your daddy who loved you more than anyone. You had your daddy who believed you were every shining loveliness that can exist in female form, a goddess of honey and beauty; even at five years old, you were the irresistible prompt for the sin of desire, so be careful who loves you. You had your daddy, a daddy who showered you when you were too old for help, but too young to understand what happened. A daddy who, when you returned from a three-day stay at a camp in upstate New Jersey, wrapped you in a private hug and whispered to make you promise that you would never leave him like that ever again. You had your daddy who told you that you were in grave danger at 13 for wearing shorts and tank tops in the summer, that men would hurt you for it, that you needed to start wearing baggy clothes if you wanted to protect yourself. A dad who cornered her in her room and physically restrained her from leaving, shouting that her boyfriend would use her for unspeakable acts, swearing that he was trying to protect her. A father who refused to meet her eyes for three days when she found her first love at 17, a father who screamed *slut* at her in the car at night even in front of her mother, a father who excommunicated her for as long as she had another man in her life. Her father, who she called when she was locked out of her car, hissing at her that she should have called her *boyfriend* if she wanted help, wasn't that what the boyfriend was there for, where oh where could the boyfriend be now that he can't help her? Maybe she should have thought that before choosing him. Her father, a ghost still living in her lungs, threatening to sink her every time she tries to breach that effervescent road where water meets the sky.

***

It is common knowledge that grasshoppers, those flying Orthopterans, are the shared prey of other winged creatures. It is true that grasshoppers retain only the intellectual distinction of detecting a predator nearby, and not its whereabouts. But has anybody ever told you why they can still maintain strong populations, even under the threat of so many predators?

Immediately as the detection of danger, grasshoppers fling themselves randomly in any of the 360° suspending them in air. Whether they fling themselves to death or safety is irrelevant.

They sense malice, and they end that life of fear, one way or another.

***

Each time I flung myself to what I hoped was safety, I found myself in a fresh turmoil that goes without a name. There is anxiety and anguish, all within an isolation so brutal it nearly knocks me off my feet, and it is a full day's work to remain standing. To be homesick is to know an alternative to this existence.

I am not so lucky, so I wrap every second tightly around my goose-pimpled flesh and squeeze my eyes shut and count memories like sheep.

Soon, I am not quite falling asleep – it is more like plummeting from a great height until my body is sprawled supine. And then I am startling awake, grasping wildly for my glasses as well as some semblance of coordinates in a hope to understand where I am in positioned in space and time.

As a child, I endured blizzards, tromped in piles of snow, built igloos to hide in when I felt petulant. I was six years old when my father brought me icey fish sticks on a paper plate, the two of us just kids misbehaving in the cold, laughing in slow motion of front of his '99 Nikon, both guilty of the need to abscond: Him to me, and me to the land.

Now, I am adapted to the desert. Temperatures of 74°F or lower cause my teeth to clack terribly together, threatening to split enamel.

I have memories, but they have been shattered as glass on brick. I wander through the dust storm proffering two hands full of broken shards to the southwest, driven only by the belief that the wind knows more than I do.

Genevieve Allaire 19

***

Three years after moving to the desert, I have become adapted to the dry heat, the dust storms, the howling wind, and the great expanse always before me. I live within a photograph of sunlight and sand, running through the same sand and rock trails, over and out, inhaling cliffs and arroyos.

Each spring carries the winds of change. Almost as soon the screaming wind, you detect that the sky is occluded with brown clouds. You can taste dirty echoes on your tongue, no matter how many windows you shut. The wind escalates its howl to a scream, rattling your windows and drowning your voice. You are as if a victim of the Dust Bowl, lungs choked with airborne particles of ground, rooting you to your grave.

Windstorms will erase desert trails, topple cairns, and pull brown wool over your face. There are no measures for when it will end or begin. Any day, we may become stranded on the highway, incapable of travel due to blindness, at the mercy of nothingness shaking our cars like an infant's toy. Unpredictably, for undetermined lengths of time, our role as emperors of land will suddenly switch to servants of the invisible force.

It is no coincidence that milestones of mine have often been interrupted by these winds of change, blasting the side of my Corolla with sand hushing me and whispering *your fault*. I never know if I will return home once caught in a dust storm.

For the winds of change have taken that, too. The winds shatter and stab me with shards of my first New Mexico home with my boyfriend who swore to protect me, piercing me with the memorials of a home fiercely expired, the day I returned to stumble upon my painted canvases thrusted into a too-small trashcan. A door left ajar, leading me to his ruby red bedsheets, still unmade, the last time he met daybreak in our shared home. Drywall with pinpricked holes from where he used to hang my drawings. A box of bullets, hollowed empty, resting on top of every photo of us I had ever printed, the last I ever saw of him before the winds took him away forever. Our matching tie-dye tank tops, the surprise that Aleve did still alleviate the *musculus iliocostalis* spasms incurred when moving three towns away. The sun blaring down on me, occluding the respite of shade, Carlsbad clouds whiter even than snow, threatening to go cumulonimbus, breezing by so high above me, taunting their escape while I stayed incarcerated to the earth. Steering off a rock-strewn road to hyperventilate, the sun impossibly bright through my eyes and into my skull. A broken promise, so many broken promises. Waking up midday to rotate supine and taste the soft rains splattering on my shelter. The drowned body soaring through freshly birthed rivers. Trucks with their flashers, grey skies, endlessly grey skies, mandatory optimism, lukewarm tequila to quell the horror bubbling over already. You are not the monster of the father of your father, killing hope with a swift kick to the gut.

But unlike the grasshopper, I returned to the point of terror. I drove three towns back, returning to Las Cruces, the town painted red with my suffering and no storms to wash it clean. I woke hours in advance of the full moon arcing over the Guadalupe Mountains, driving in stasis, numb even as border inspection searched my car with canines for proof of crime. The corruption against myself was legal, much to the border inspection agent's sleepy summer chagrin. I drove as a statue, expressionless, fueled on four hours' sleep to make the six-hour round trip more bearable. I chose to wear baggy clothes at the gas station before I ventured into the unknown expanse between homes, so that men would not want to hurt me, as my daddy taught me. Hefting disassembled furniture from my sedan and into a discount 5'x 5' x 5' storage locker, no witnesses as I heaved my childhood bed frame into an adjacent landfill, and pressing *0529 into the exit keypad, granted absconce with a *"Thank you, ________ ___! YOU MAY EXIT"* reverberating within my neurons' most permanent synapses as I drove in low gear into a new roommate situation in rural pecan orchards, tromped into photographic memory as dirt roads and neighbors cautiously stealing a glance at me behind bonfires as I trip through my familiar locomotion into miles indefinite that I would take black in the pre-morning. Silent fabric masks, a university parking sticker — a new one, for my PhD — that took the place of the one to get my master's, that I used to understand as a sacrifice of hope, pummeling my once life-bearing guts. Running well before sunrise, running into darkness and private property, illuminated by my flashlight or else the static headlights of a pecan harvesting truck taking a pre-sunrise siesta, me as a ground dweller running for simple survival, hoping in vain to outpace the trailing pesticide planes, to feel some sense of belonging in this alien world, the same world that mauled me and took me back, carving me with a torso that collapsed concave. running from night into daybreak, to turn this grief into some semblance of grace. Repeating to myself, over and over again, that this made sense. This would be good. This would be home.

But it never was.

***

It occurred to me, last summer in the dizzying heat of an unincorporated pecan orchard, that while I have shed religion as much as I felt able, some pains would always feel deserved: Penance. That is how I felt then, in my bedroom, 86°F and climbing. 86°F is far too low for heat stress, but regardless of the numbers, it was dizzying. Dizzying to fold laundry, dizzying even to lay down. Better to try to eat salt. A good indicator of gauging potential hyponatremia was letting the crystals dissolve on my tongue, wait to see if it tasted good, if it was something I craved.

Yes, penance, I thought, seated on my mattress, completely unmoving. Fans whirled above me in vain, the kind of naivety I wished I could smash like the bugs on the quilt the night before. These fans, spinning senselessly, blades at odd angles, pull cords made of shoelaces and snapped metal beading, light fixtures quaking ominously. How could it go on day and night, shaking so terribly, not simply cracking and plummeting to its death?

It has to be penance, I thought, sweat soaking through my freshly laundered shirt. Everything had to do with surviving the infinite seconds, minutes, hours of this day. And the next, and then, every other day after that one. It was impossible to think that it was only 4:00 PM: That I would be awake for six more hours. How? How is there space enough for me to exist for six more hours before sleep takes me and It will only if it feels merciful. Still there will be the nightmares. The rapidly beating heart that begins sometimes around 5:00 AM most mornings, pushing to me the blindness of pre-sunrise in pecan orchards, impossible to placate no matter how many miles you search with your flashlight beam bobbing, synchronized with the rise and fall of your lungs, arcing over yourself as the Guadalupes, a moon reflecting light never belonging to itself, but yours for the stealing if you were sharp about it.

Take it every breath, one at a time, tuned to the metronome of a second hand. Here was a second. If you say it all at once, the second hand will make its way past the *2* and back to the *2* on the same rotation, so that your recollection cannot take up more space than the 360°spread across the 0.10 m² ahead of you, sixty seconds confined to the one logical tune of time which measures your sentence.

But one minute can stretch all the way out into eternity, so be smart about seeing yourself back.

***

Trail running through unpopulated desert is a serious game with high stakes if you lose, yet it remains the one thing that makes sense in this new reality, where I live new days with old trauma. The trails I find are blind to somebody who is not rooted firmly to this particular *terra firma*. Arroyos and cliffs meander to intersections of bare trail, which precipitate like snares in a spider's web.

I must focus on studying and interpreting the vast shrublands before me; my very survival depends on it. Even when the sun beats on me like a hammer, I must find a way to connect the *here* and the *not*. Fear has no place here: I entertain only the incorporation of Life into these wretched bones, nurturing me to effervesce these tunes of truth to you.

When I run in land that has claimed my body, a sacrifice to the knowledge of heat that will set you free, I don't dare divert my gaze. I don't think too much. I am here for the task of abscoinding – so abscond.

I drag my heels in the sand to mark my initials in the great expanse, a sign that not even wildfire smoke can obscure. Sunrise sheds eager pink streaks to my east, the stars to the west blinking away nighttime's blind cast. Jackrabbits leap away from my impending step, and Datura flowers begin to fold in on themselves. Pastels give way to the blue illumination of day, and I retrace my steps to run back home.

The Guadalupe Mountains rest upon millions of years. No matter how many times I have passed through them – through monsoons, flash floods, dust storms, the blindness of night – it feels like the ghost of my suffering may feel infinite. *Infinite* is not the same as *indefinite*. But what do these distinctions mean to life like mountains? Millions of years, or moments all lined up indefinitely: Whose warden dictates the length of the sentence?

When my brain and my body have been wrung clean by the sun, I soar through the rolling hills, driven home to myself every time.

Here, and then not.

Cynthia Singerman

Negative Space

I arrive at the stone circle at dawn. The grass, still coated with ice, crunches beneath my feet. The woods are black and bare, and I shiver beneath my down jacket. It is too cold to snow, too cold to be out walking, but it is Christmas Eve and I am going to lay the wreath by the stones. The ones I placed there all those years ago. It's strange how rituals begin and then take hold, because it's been almost twenty years since Will's been gone.

We first walked these woods in the springtime and white wildflowers dotted the grass.

"I love white flowers. Something about the brightness against the green," I told him. "Like little snow blossoms."

"I'll remember that," Will said.

He always remembered everything I told him, how I wanted to be a professor like my father. Now, I work at a college not far from the college where my father works. In academia, someone always knows someone and I was hired by a friend of a friend of my father's. First as an assistant, then as an adjunct. I got tenure this year—and it was like hitting the jackpot, winning the lottery. It actually is in our profession. I know I got lucky. I have connections. I could be one of those ridiculous jerks who claims that they had to work even harder to prove themselves because of their connections but I'm not. My father looms larger than life as the Foreign Language department chair. He's eighty now, but won't retire. Every year he tells me he's considering it, but then changes his mind.

"I just can't do it Loma," he says. "Where would I go?" He gestures to the stacks of books and piles of papers. "What would I do?" He strokes his beard, something he acquired in his later years, and it's a wild fury of silver.

"Read, hike," I rack my brain for possibilities. "Date."

"Ha." He shrugs. "I do all of those things already."

"Yes, but you would have more time. You could relax."

"I'll think about it."

I don't think he does.

A blast of wind whistles through the naked branches and my eyes sting with tears. I am sure my nose will be bright pink when I return home. And it is, when I slip off my knitted hat and hang my coat on the old wooden carved rack by our front door, pausing in front of my reflection, desperate to ignore the silver strands in my light brown hair. How time marches on, year after year despite my silent protests. I don't linger long though. Quinn is calling for me.

"Mama, mama. I need help with my hair."

I feel grateful I am still needed, because she is ten. In two years, she will probably find me dull. She'll turn up her nose at our game nights and reading hours, dashing out the door to meet her friends. Or maybe I'll get lucky and she'll tolerate me through her teenage years. She's an only child, like I was, so maybe she'll be like I was, always more comfortable at home, talking to my father while curled under a flannel blanket. But I know it is futile to imagine my daughter will be anything like me. She is a butterfly, batting her wings, fluttering about from one group to the next.

"Are you nervous to start school?" I ask her every year.

"No of course not Mama," she says seriously. "Everyone loves me."

It's true. Everyone loves Quinn. She's charming and funny. A star gymnast, coordinated and competitive in ways that are absolutely outrageous considering I'm her mother. She must get it from Jordan, her father, who loves to dance. He's a professor, like me and teaches with my father. We are actually a lot alike. Will and I were nothing alike. But it was still perfect. The past can always be perfect if you want it to be.

The other night I found a list tucked in Quinn's down jacket pocket. *Addison Godfrey Jake Colton Mrs. Loonis Matilda's Dad's New Girlfriend*

"Quinn," I ask her. "What is this?"

"My revenge list," she says. Her eyes round like saucers, brimming with innocence. "Not for right now, but just so I can keep track."

I sigh.

"Don't worry Mama. It's not a kill list or anything."

I bite my lip, fighting a smile. "What did Matilda's Dad's new girlfriend do?"

"Oh," Quinn says. "She's the reason Mattie's parents got divorced."

"Hmmm."

Later, I crawl into bed with Jordan and put my cold feet on his warm calves.

"Jesus Loma," he yowls. "They're like ice."

I ignore him. "Can you not let Quinn watch *Game of Thrones* with you please? That show is not for kids."

He makes a noise like a *hmm-mmm*, then rolls toward me, kisses me lightly and then rolls back, instantly asleep. I stay awake, listening to the wind, staring into the blackness outside our window. Finally, I get up and go to my study to open the box I took from my father's house three months ago. I read Will's letters over and over again even though I already know the words by heart. I stare intently at our photographs, as if by committing these images to memory I will be transported back there. Eventually, I close my eyes, slipping into a restless sleep. When I wake, it's still dark, the house still quiet, the photo still clutched between my fingers.

"You're up early," Jordan says now, as Quinn comes tumbling down the stairs towards me. "How was your walk?"

His tone seems borderline accusatory. It is this new thing we're doing, passive-aggressive bait. *What does that mean* I could say and Jordan would respond with *Nothing*. And I'll say *Whatever*. Is this how marriages fall apart? Death by a thousand snide remarks. I don't know—I know I don't want a divorce. But I seem intent on self-sabotage. I've begun to slip away, lost in these moments in my mind that will never come again.

"Loma," Jordan starts to say something else but stops. He touches the tip of my nose. "Your father called—he's on his way."

"Yay!" Quinn claps her hands together, squealing with delight. My father spends Christmas Eve with us—we make cookies: *Speculoos, Vanillekipferi*. My father cooks salmon with roasted potatoes and spends the night so we can all wake up on Christmas Day together. We drink *gluwein*. and play whatever games Quinn chooses.

"I put the dove on the top of the tree Mama," Quinn is saying now. "It looks better that way." She smiles at me like we share a secret and lowers her voice. "It's my favorite because you're my favorite."

I stop braiding her hair, trying not to cry. *Please don't leave me*, I think. *Please*, I beg.

"Mama! Keep braiding." Quinn prattles on. Her voice is a lulling thrum in my ears until she says something that turns my mouth dry. "I didn't know people used to call you Dove Monday."

That's because they didn't. Only one person ever did.

My parents named me Paloma. It means dove in Spanish. They picked Paloma because I was conceived on their honeymoon. They always believed it had to be Granada. I went there to study in college, walking through the winding paths of the *Albaicin*, smoking hashish cigarettes and drinking red wine in the plazas. Where Lorca once sat by the river and wrote. I was a romantic back then.

My last name is Montag. It means Monday in German. Paloma Montag. Or Dove Monday. And I was bird-like, but not elegant and precious like a dove. More like small and forgettable, like a finch. I have a face like a thousand other people, brown hair like my mother. She didn't speak Spanish, but my father did. He loved to shock people with it, shock them with his shock of bright blonde hair and piercing blue eyes, a tall, broad man with a booming voice. He spoke with a perfect accent in English, German, and Spanish, having gone to an American High School in Germany. But I think they named me Paloma after my mother. Delicate, beautiful, with a voice like golden silk. Me, I can sing, but I always preferred to be hidden away in a tower among piles of books and research.

Will was the one who called me Dove Monday. We met my sophomore year. His senior year. I was in the library wearing my glasses and my mother's old LL Bean sweater. Cream and cable knit.

"What are you working on?"

These are his first words to me. He looks like Al Pacino in *The Godfather*. His coat was Armani and he drove a BMW. "I like my clothes Italian and my cars German," Will used to say. I found his arrogance intoxicating. Someone like him could love someone like me.

"I'm writing a paper." I say.

"About what?"

I can see the burnished gold flecks in his green eyes. His gaze, breaks me open, swiftly and sharply like the crack of an egg on the side of silver bowl, the thick liquid spilling out from the shell.

"A man sentenced to death because he doesn't cry at his mother's funeral."

I am trying to impress him, even though pretty much everyone reads *The Stranger*. But he sits and listens to me explain my paper. After, we go for a walk. It is late and cold but I go anyway because I would have gone anywhere with him. He kisses me and I can hear the river rushing by us. I believed Will would always be the same boy who kissed me by the river, who would visit me in Paris, and that's how he remains.

But maybe he wasn't. I'll never know.

The last time I saw Will we were sitting in the airport lounge waiting at the gate. The cold, air-conditioned room raised goose bumps on my skin and Will draped his gray hoodie around my shoulders. His hands rest there, heavy and reassuring and I smile up at him, grateful. My two sweaters were packed in my suitcase, checked for my flight to Madrid, not necessary for the steamy August day. Outside, the air rippled from the jet fumes. It was a parting gift for the long flight, smelling slightly of his arctic fresh deodorant with traces of cologne. I won't give it back, I think, when in just eight weeks we would meet in Paris. But we never went to Paris, at least not together.

I still dream of the trip we never took. Will and I walking along the Seine at midnight and watching the shimmering lights on the water. In the morning, the grass is so green beneath our backs as we nap under the Eiffel tower. The sky is so blue it glows above us. But it's only a dream.

A month later, one day after my twentieth birthday I wake in my twin bed with a headache, a faint pulsing in my left temple. It was past noon and the sunlight sliced through the window like a sword, blinding me with a brilliant yellow flare because I forgot to close the blinds.

The night before I'd celebrated with my roommate Marta in *Sacromonte*, listening to a flamenco guitar and drinking wine in the candlelit caves. I danced, pirouetting with happiness in my new Zara pants, tight and cherry red. Marta hemmed them for me, nearly half a foot, because the clothes were for Spanish women, who were all so tall and sleek and slender, smoking their cigarettes in high-heeled boots. We'd arrived home late, and I lay in bed, staring at the thumbtacked pictures of Will and me while I placed my foot on the floor to stop the room from spinning. Just one month until Paris, I think. One month.

I remember every single detail of that day after my birthday, so much more than my actual birthday, which is September 10th. I'm a Virgo. My father is also a Virgo—his birthday on September 9th, which is the most common birthday in the world. I'm not one for astrology, but my mother was. *I'm a Sagittarius, I can't stay in one place.* She would say. *You two are like peas in your Virgo pods. I don't belong.* Her convenient crutch for her selfish behavior. It wasn't written in the stars, she just did whatever it was that she wanted to do. And she did not want to be tied to a cold, snowy existence, with a professor and his stacks of books and the needs of her daughter. Will was a Libra. *I'm a Libra and I like to draw.* He loved this brief biographical statement about himself, as if it summed up everything there was to know about him in two phrases. I have the last drawing he sent me, a pencil sketch of the Eiffel tower. Maybe he would rather have been sketching then working all hours at a financial services firm. But he loved his job. He loved New York. He was born and raised there—his father a gorgeous Italian party boy and his mother a rebellious WASP until her father threatened to cut her off. *Then away went my father*, he says, lying next to me, tangled up in his sheets the color of faded denim from when he washed a navy sock with his whites. How it was just Will and his older sister Elise, in this huge brownstone. How he would stay in his sister's room and dance to *Forever Your Girl* because they'd stolen the cassette from their au pair. He laughs as if he knew he should be embarrassed but wasn't.

Now you tell me something, he says, but I can never think of anything comparable to share. All my memories feel burdensome or boring. *I had a rescue dog named Floki. He and my father were my only friends. The Danish is actually from Germany, not Denmark.* So instead, I just say, *my mother died in a fire.*

That was a lie. My parents divorced when I was ten. My mother left to wander the world and never came back. I saved her postcards until one day I burned them all, watching the paper dissolve into dust in the flames. And I created another version of a mother, another version of my life, and I would tell myself this story enough times until it almost felt true.

That day in Granada, the day after my birthday, I remember my hangover was not of the unpleasant variety. In fact, as I made my way through the streets, the day had a soothing malaise to it. The weather was warm, and I wore a gauzy dress that swished around my ankles as I walked. In my woven bag was a notebook and a story collection by Ana Maria Matute. I buy a large café con leche and a donut dusted with cinnamon sugar. I smoke Fontana Lights with two girls from my program outside the Internet Café where I check my email twice a week

Then I sit sipping my coffee as I log into my Hotmail account. I think back at how slow things moved, even then, when I thought everything moved so fast. There were still messages on answering machines, missed connections, days without staring at a screen.

If only, I think. If only I had called Will that morning, so he would be the one to stop for a coffee, make him wait just a little while longer to chat, be late just this once. If only I had sensed something that could have protected him.

But I didn't. Instead I was blissfully unaware that as I opened the birthday e-card Will had sent me, life would be irreparably shattered. On the screen were two cats, their tails intertwined underneath a crescent moon and blinking stars on a navy sky. Will had typed out the lyrics from a love song in yellow sans-serif font. He loved sappy, over the top romantic gestures—things that now would make me cringe. A scavenger hunt across campus for our anniversary, a journal he kept for writing notes to me. He had sent the e-card the night before, while it was still my birthday in New York.

What I remember next was the commotion. Exclamations and this sweeping sense that something terrible was happening. Circles gathered outside. People clutching their hands, mouths gaping open. *There's been an attack* someone said. *The Twin Towers.* But we could not figure out exactly what was going on. I didn't even have a television—the chaos was a world away. *He must be okay.* I repeat this to myself like a prayer. He had to be. His card is still open on my computer screen.

I run outside then, shivering in the late afternoon sun, my teeth chattering. I was disappearing, wondering if I would faint, the edges of my vision wavering black and brown. I didn't though, I just stand there, paralyzed, a vile, sour taste in my mouth from the remnants of coffee and bile rising in my throat. People follow me, asking me if I was okay but I can't speak. I didn't know how—in English, Spanish. I muttered something in German, my first language, the language of my father, before I turned and walked away.

I walk and walk, pacing the city. The night fell and it was close to midnight when I finally reached my father. The streets were still very much alive in Granada, people gathering for dinner and drinks. Errant laughter, bits of broken conversation floated by on a light breeze.

"Loma," he says. Then he tells me.

Will was already buried under a thousand tons of dust and ashes. I thought of the postcards I'd burned from my mother and how some of us must continue living while the ones we love are dead.

When I flew home in December, we hit turbulence somewhere over the Atlantic. The woman sitting next to me clutched the armrest, her knuckles bright white as she let out small, shallow whimpers. It was unbearable. I took her hand, sweaty and soft, her thick diamond wedding band digging into my palm. It left a dark blood blister, blackish purple, rimmed red. *Thank you*, she says later as we exit, her eyes moist, watery blue. *I'm just so scared to fly now.* I nod, not really sure what I'm agreeing with, but I have nothing else to say.

There was no one to greet me at the gate. There was just a winding maze of signs and security until I reached the baggage claim where my father was waiting. I wore Will's gray sweatshirt but it didn't smell anything like him any more. It smelled like my own perspiration and cigarette smoke and the funk of buses and trains and planes. Still, I refused to wash it, as if the detergent and warm water would rinse away Will's touch, erase a scent that no longer existed. My father hugged me and his hug felt the way it always felt, warm and safe and reassuring that everything would be okay, even when it never would.

At home, I curl up in my childhood bed, still wearing Will's sweatshirt, and watch TV. Endless hours of the news cycles I did not see in Spain. Images of the flames, the falling towers, the people jumping rather than drowning in piles of rubble. Faces covered in soot and ash. The screaming and crying. I watch until my eyelids pulse from the artificial light and my head throbs from staring at the screen. I relive Will's death a thousand times, unable to sleep until I take the pills I bought from the Spanish pharmacy, over the counter, like candy.

After the fourth day in bed my father comes into my room. It is Christmas Eve.

"Loma," he says. "Will you sit with me in the kitchen?" Even in the depths of my despair, I cannot deny my father. I sit on a wooden stool and watch him bake for what seems like hours. I smell like overripe lemons—pungent.

When he speaks, his voice is gentle. "Sometimes we get through hard things simply one day at a time. One foot in front of the other." He gave me the journal, the one with the letters Will wrote to me, the one Will's mother had given my father to give to me. "Letting go doesn't mean forgetting. But if we hold something too tightly, it will consume us."

That was when we went for our walk, our footsteps leaving fresh prints in the soft snow. The midnight sky negative space between the burning stars. We walk until we got to the clearing where I went with Will. I place the circle of stones, the ones Will had once placed upon paper clues on our college campus, leading me back to him.

I kept every single thing he'd ever given me—the shell earrings that shone like opals, the letters, the dried flowers. Our journal. I took it all, took every single memory, every photo and put it in the box. It was the only way. They were my drugs I would get high on every day if I'd had my way, only to come crashing down, shaking, needing my next fix. Never moving on.

I was in graduate school when I met Jordan. It was my father's annual holiday party and I wore a silk dress and gold jewelry. My hair pulled back off my face. We all drank glass after glass of mulled wine and Jordan and I danced to *Have Yourself a Merry Little Christmas*. He kissed me goodbye and his glasses fogged from our breath. We married that summer and went to Cote d'Azur, then Paris for our honeymoon. I bought a postcard of the Blue Nude from the Matisse museum and Rondini sandals to wear with my white sundress. We drank rosé with lunches of *boullibaisse*. There was a slowness to the days, something that for me resembled contentment.

In Paris, Jordan asked if I wanted to hang a lock with our initials. He grinned, happy, relaxed. His skin was very tan from the beach, his brown hair long and curling over the collar of his shirt.

I shook my head. "No. I don't like that sappy stuff."

But I can't help thinking of Will. And on our last day when Jordan is engrossed in a book, I walk to the *Pont des Arts*, putting the lock with Will's name and mine before throwing away the key.

"Where did you go?" Jordan asks. It is a question he will ask me again and again, but I never tell him. I never tell anyone.

I could have told my father. I could tell him today as I watch his car pull into the driveway. But I am too ashamed—my destructive addiction to Will rearing its ugly head.

"Opa is here! Opa is here!" Quinn whoops and cartwheels through the living room, narrowly missing a lamp with her foot.

My father greets me with a hug and kiss before asking, "are you alright?" in a low whisper. Our eyes meet.

"I'm fine. Papa. Great." I laugh. He sighs and clucks his tongue. But then Quinn dives into his arms, diverting his attention. I retreat, fade into the background as our traditional Christmas Eve commences.

Later, I watch Quinn as she plays dominos with my father before my gaze drifts to the Christmas tree, to the blinking yellow lights. I stare for so long a halo forms around the lights that spreads out, distorting my sight. I think of my reflection after this morning's walk. My pale sallow complexion, the sharp lines surrounding the bluish, purple half moons underneath my eyes. My body, my being, decaying with each passing second. I could feel myself, heavy with age. The brittle bones beneath my sagging skin, my spine curving as I sink slowly towards death. And in my mind, I see the photograph of me and Will and wonder if this was truly the same life.

I avoid my father's look as I get up and walk to the study. I can't stop myself as I go straight to the box, to the journal and the photo inside—a selfie taken with a disposable camera—and I study it once more. Will and I are both flushed with rosy cheeks, so full of life. My throat burns for these lost souls—and finally see how maybe I was beautiful, my hair gleaming, my teeth white, my skin so smooth with youth. I see myself so differently now, through the lens of all these years gone by.

I glance up. Jordan is in the doorway watching me.

"What is this?" He asks calmly. Kindly even. Because Jordan is kind and calm and if I told him about Will, he would probably understand. But then I would have to share. I would have to let go. And I can't.

"My stuff," I say defensively.

"I see that."

He takes off his glasses and wipes the lenses, slowly, with intention. I know this habit. It's what he does when Quinn's done something bad. It's what he does when he's testing his students on their dissertations.

"Are you having an affair with a dead person?"

I see now that he already knows. And we live in an age where there are no secrets, nothing stays hidden. A few clicks on the computer and you can find out anything and everything about anyone. I wonder what Quinn knows then, when she said my name this morning. What she's heard or seen or read.

A kind of rot begins to pass through my stomach, the hot sensation right before you get sick. I swallow and clutch the photo tighter between my sweaty fingers.

"This is private." I'm panicked. My tone shrill. "Private."

"Loma," Jordan says. "Please. Talk to me."

"Leave me alone."

And I flee, brushing by him, sprinting to grab my coat and bolt out the door.

I know what my father said to me, about holding things too tightly. But what if that is the only way for me to keep him? To make sure Will belongs the most to me? He might fade away completely, if I don't cling to these memories with superhuman strength.

I run to the stones, where I stop, dizzy from the burst of exercise and for a moment I think I see Will, standing in the snow, his dark hair uncombed, tall, shivering in just a t-shirt. I can touch him, I know I can, solid and young and frozen in time. *Don't you know I'm always here* he whispers, *I've never left.* I fall deeper and deeper into this imaginary world of the past until I almost forget what is real, what is the now. He holds out his hand, and I take it, his grip like ice. The cold creeps through my fingers, numbing me. His arm looping around my waist, the ecstasy of his touch encircles me like a dream. I want it so badly, this feeling of being with him. I want to stay here, in this magical land of make-believe. Not living, not dead.

I hear the rustling of footsteps behind me and I turn, expecting to see Jordan but it's not.

"Mama."

It's Quinn. Her red hat beaming like a stoplight under the bright white moon. Stop, I think. I must stop.

"Sweetie, what are you doing out here?"

She rushes to me, flinging her arms around me, squeezing me so it is hard to breathe. But I am breathing, as is Quinn, panting like a wild animal, so alive in my embrace. She is warm, still smelling of the burning wood from our fire and the cinnamon of the scented candles.

"I followed you." Her face is buried in my coat. "I was worried."

"Oh Sweet-pea I'm so sorry." I hate that I caused her pain, even though it is inevitable that I will again at some point, no matter what I wish or want, because these things are beyond my control. So much is beyond my control and yet, so much I know, deep down, is in my grasp. Tears spring to my eyes, a swelling in my throat and my chest.

"What are you doing Mama? You're so cold."

She presses one of her gloved hands to my throat. In my haste to run away I did not wear a scarf and my neck is bare. I've never worn jewelry, not like Quinn, who wears piles of them, layers upon layers. I think of another memory then, of Quinn, all her necklaces tangled together and I can't get them unstuck. *You're doing it wrong Mama,* she shrieks, her cheeks hot and wet with tears. *No, no, no!* My hands shake and I want to scream with frustration and Jordan comes in, presses his hand to my back and takes over, deftly unwinding the jumble of gold and silver and beads.

"Mama?" she asks again. "What are you doing?"

I think of the Christmas music playing back at the house, my father on another glass of *gluwein.* Jordan, patiently waiting, probably eating another cookie.

"I don't know," I say finally.

I stroke her hair and let her hold me.

"It's too cold out here." She takes my hand. "We have to go back now."

I nod. This invented place where I escape, it is not for the living. Quinn pulls me, and I look back, just once, but the clearing is empty.

And then the snow begins to fall, landing softly on the green of the spruce trees, They look like white wildflowers in springtime.

Emma Jahoda-Brown

Donor

Like a fine tomato the organ was wrapped in tissue
    I drove to the hospital with the windows down

and the heat on yes I'm not who I thought I was busy
    choosing groceries impatient in the line at Giant it moved
slowly then forked

I heard the news by the magazines when the mind goes blank there
is the body
    circuits firing like sparklers all the cedar towers couldn't
quench

so they say he never spoke above a whisper
    he liked the myrtle ear trumpet that it is shallow and only
hears blue tones

in desperate times he played the piano loved objets trouvés and
impermanence
    his daughter takes refuge in a folding chair her face like a
sticky bun

after it's over I use the medical scissors I slipped in my bag
    to cut open a bag of potatoes I think of the things he will
never touch

but you will — crystalized sugar dyed hair keypads the beating goes
on in you
    like a sudden drizzle your blood the smell of collected pennies

Kathie Collins

The Home Depot

I invent reasons to go: urgent needs like light
bulbs, window cleaner, hooks for pictures
I never get around to hanging, cans of high gloss,
apple-red paint to spray the wicker on the porch—
next weekend for sure. Which is why I find myself

here on aisle one, remembering the late winter sun
rising over the cow pasture, the way it catches
a sparrow's wing tips and the corner of the barn,
sets white-washed boards aglow as Dad and I cross
the yard to open his cabinet shop for the day.

Above me on aisle two, fluorescent bulbs buzz—
and I flip the switch to set Dad's shop
lights humming. I listen to the band-saw whir
as it makes its first cut of the day, try to swing
the smallest of his hammers, watch curlicues

of white pine fall like snow behind the planer
as he guides through board after long board,
while I perch on his drafting stool dreaming,
my whole life spread before me. I breathe in
his world: machine oil, turpentine-soaked rags,

carpenter's glue. And beneath it all, fragrance
of pine and poplar, hickory, walnut—a forest
that still beckons, begs me to linger a little longer
in Lumber, to lean on the cart handle recalling
my first home in his flannel-shirted arms, his smile

at the center of a dark beard covered in dust
sanded from the same woods that will one day
form a box to hold my body. I am lucky

to be a cabinet maker's daughter.
The box will feel like home.

Matt Cheek

Thomas

Let destruction come upon him at unawares; and let his net that he hath hid catch himself: into that very destruction let him fall. – Psalms 35:8

Doc McCormack is kneeling in a pool of blood up to his ankles trying to save what is remaining of Thomas' leg. Doc's face is paved under a layer of camo paint, blood, and dirt. I parrot my combat lifesaver training, clearing Thomas' airway and applying pressure to his neck wound. More than a million miles of veins and blood flow out of his lower extremities, where Doc is working furiously. Laid end to end these morsels of human life would stretch to the moon and back. And all of it is shitty with the smell of phosphorus. The neck wound I throw some QuickClot onto, the way it smells mixed with the cigarette smoke makes me tired and makes my heart pound. Maybe I'm a little out of my head. The ammonia, the smoke, the emails my parents keep sending about my sister's latest abusive boyfriend. I don't dare reply to the emails. I know for sure I'll never care about anything ever again.

Star light and the waning moon makes faint shadows of our silhouettes out in the open desert. Sgt. Smith spots movement near an outcropping of rock and sees a man crawling among the strewn and tumbled boulders. The man is crawling not even 40 yards from where we are working on Thomas' torn body which lies bleeding into the desert sand. Sgt. Smith squeezes off a round from his M203 grenade launcher at the rag of a man tumbling towards escape across the slate. The grenade impacts on a rock right near the man's face and his movement stops among the flames and ensuing cloud of dust. The body laid there for a while after as we continued to try to save Thomas. As the remaining embers extinguish, Sgt. Smith retrieves the man's head and mangled neck. The charred skin pulled taut; the eyes cooked in their sockets. I sit scanning the landscape for some guidance in the emptiness, ignoring my friend Thomas as he dies slowly beneath me - both a victim and an agent of his own, young death. Sgt. Smith later displayed the enemy's head gruesomely on a low hanging branch outside of our patrol base from holes he'd created just behind the ears. The head hung there for weeks blackened, swollen, and strange and many times daily we trudged past it to perform our patrols.

***

Do not kill each other or yourselves. Surely Allah is ever Merciful to you. - Surah 4:29

"Have you had any outbursts lately?" The therapist asks. "Have you had any incidents that you would describe as out of control or disconnected from reality?"

The way the therapist sits there asking me stuff with her mouth halfway clamped around a cigarette reminds me of the way detainees would sit there trying to choke down water after several days without it – almost shaking with hatred in their eyes and staring at you. A sip, a smirk, a question – breathing, drinking, and asking. They demonstrate all the basic applications of a human mouth. But we Marines see these detainees as less than human. During the deployment Lt. Collier was asked to put down Dickweed, third platoon's dog they stole from a house we raided in Musa Qala. Lt. Collier couldn't bring himself to kill Dickweed, even though the dog was barely able to eat or drink anything due to the amount of presumed cancer or something that had overtaken his frail body.

Eventually Sgt. Smith shot the dog and threw his body over a cliff. Greason filmed the whole thing on his GoPro and finds it hilarious to show us all how far the dog's splatter spread across the sandy knoll beneath them after Smith hurled its lifeless corpse. Later that evening Lt. Collier shot a detainee in the face with his service pistol without the slightest hesitation. The detainee had his arms zip-tied behind his back. Once his limp body spilled onto the floor, the blood poured from his head at an astounding rate. Doc McCormack saw Collier shoot the detainee – thereby committing a war crime. Doc looked at me as if something invisible had just punched him in the face. I think we were just ashamed of ourselves but disgusted with one another as we entered into a dark and terrible covenant.

Matt Cheek **43**

Early on in this mental rehabilitation program they tried to babysit all the veterans of the war in Afghanistan with medication. Xanax, Prozac, Valium, Imipramine – the plan crashed because too many veterans tried to hold their prescriptions for three weeks, six weeks, eight weeks – depending on their body weight and then down their stash with a scotch chaser to kill themselves swiftly and silently.

Suicides are common among us who survived our fight, nearly 20 per day. They appear to happen in waves, Marines and Soldiers falling head-first into a fistful of pills like lemmings following one another off a cliff's edge. I fight off the urge to follow by constantly reminding myself that I am numb to everything I experienced – ultimately forgetting that numbness implies that the feeling will one day return.

***

While I'm busy treating the wound on Thomas' upper extremities, Doc McCormack is asking me something, but I don't reply. I'm muttering to myself "Improvised explosive device. Femoral artery collapse. Sucking chest wound." I'm categorizing Thomas into his appropriate category of death. I like to divide the dead in my head based on the manner of death – creating facets, categories, and metadata for each entry into the death repository.

I realize I haven't paid enough attention to the sucking chest wound Thomas is suffering from. His face turns pale as I reach into the Velcro sealed, back section of his plate carrier and find the 8"x10" photo of his wife and daughter that he carries back there for good luck and tape the photo over the chest wound to prevent the wound from fully collapsing his lungs, causing him to choke to death on his own blood. Generally, deaths can be categorized across multiple facets – sight, sound, smell, and manner. The sounds associated with death are usually a full-throated cry for one's parental unit followed by giving up, a mule-like sound, or pathetic whimpers such as those that emanate from a dog toy. Though the outcome of every death, civilian or Marine, is ultimately the same – the efforts to save the life of a Marine and to then clean up after you've failed is a whole production. Though they are all dead, they

exist neither in heaven nor hell, they are inventory in my mental
rolodex of death.

After maybe thirty minutes of Doc and I trying to save his life,
Thomas succumbs to his wounds and dies. Everything that was
supposed to be red turns blue – his lips, his eyelids, his tongue. I
start to think of my life as a sick joke. A victim of global politics
and posturing. What do you call the Marine who honorably served?
Dead. What do you call his friend who carefully zipped up his body
in a thick, black bag? Dead. What do you call a has-been who
performed his final act of importance at twenty years of age? Dead.
Later that week we have a small memorial service for Thomas
before we take off on the next round of daily patrols. The chaplain
begins the ceremony by reminding us all of the fragility of life – as
if we needed a reminder. If Thomas had not stepped on a pressure
plate IED, regardless of his intentions, maybe he would also be at
this ceremony. The chaplain then begins to read from the Bible. In
some bizarre screw up, he says he's reading a verse from the book
of Psalms, but actually reads from the book of Lamentations: *Mine
eyes do fail with tears, my bowels are troubled, my liver is poured upon the earth,
for the destruction of the daughter of my people.* Nobody notices or cares.

Lillo Way

Etudes: Tacit

Listen to the quiet. No one
has awakened, cleared the throat,
gargled, spat, slammed off the faucet,
peed a powerful cataract
into what was a calm white pond.
The refrigerator is still asleep.
I've shut off the furnace,
and am blessedly speechless.
Exhausted by early exuberance,
the birds nap. A slight smile
bears up the sags of my lower face.
Oh the glorious nothing of it.
If silence exists only in death,
I'll make a grand dead person.

———————

For bird song, or even bird chat. Not
for anything else would I trade silence.
Not the ting of a finger cymbal. Not
even Mozart, and certainly not
for a word. But if there must be words,
let them be in some other language,
a flowing one, one that susurrates,
that says *hush, sough*, a sibilant *shush*.
Tide rushing through small pebbles.
Love songs of the wood thrush. Swoosh
of a window fan on a summer day.
Crush of quince petals under bare feet.
Pliant maple leaves, silk skirts
in a breeze.

How will the old ones tell us
about the silent half
of the word grief? By wearing
black? Absence of color.
Would they offer us
the letter O? Empty space
in a spider web, hole
where a thread broke. How is it
these two men, so old, are still alive?
What are they whispering to each other,
sitting there in heavy woolens
on the park bench?
Could their lips be moving
soundlessly?

____

how still
the birch trunks
the thousand small leaves
silent among them
as they surround
one
tall thin spire
branchless birdless
in a clearing
motionless as a corpse
where I
a stranger
will refrain
from entering

Leslie Parker

American Polaroid

I see them in two-tone,
my parents, their friends,
not in sepia
like my grandparents' generation,
not gnarl-fingered, not fish-eyed
as they are now,
but as they were
in 1961, on the shy side of forty,
slipped from the bonds of the workweek,
entertaining themselves
on an occasional Saturday night,
with chips,
Lipton's onion soup dip,
a highball or two,
Bennett, Sinatra and Peggy Lee
pouring from the hi-fi,
men in crisp shirts,
faces lit with laughter, women
rustling in taffeta petticoats,
pearls beading their throats,
cigarette holders poised
with a Lucky Strike,
looking for a light.

Bill Colvard

Breakfast at Bubba's

At nine o'clock in the morning, the oppressive heat and humidity of New York in August had already begun to vaporize the shimmering oil-slicked puddles of dog piss accumulating on North Moore Street. Carolyn Beck splurged on a cab to bring her down to TriBeCa that morning because she didn't want to wear her brand-new Louboutins on the subway. Carolyn always felt a neighborhood as glamorous as TriBeCa demanded her finest footwear, even on the weekend, but TriBeCa's grit was an integral part of its glamour, and that grit— in the form of broken sidewalks and cobblestones which readily harbored the urine streams of a profusion of overbred pooches in Hermès collars—was about to result in more of a challenge to her crimson-soled stilettos than the Number Six train could possibly have presented.

Carolyn and her business partner both commuted from less fashionable parts of town, she from Yorkville, and he from an area of Flatbush that remained stubbornly resistant to gentrification. They pooled their meager resources to pay the exorbitant rent on an office in the land of glamour and grit: a miniature loft with one minuscule window overlooking a cobblestone alley beloved by television location scouts as a repository for dead bodies on procedural dramas. It was an unspoken article of faith between them that setting up shop in a part of town where everybody was known to have fuck-you money would make them appear invincible to future clients and current creditors. Two years in, their hopes had yet to be realized.

The cab lurched to a stop a few feet from the intersection of Hudson and North Moore. Carolyn shoved two twenties through the glass partition, telling the driver to keep the change. She judged the appropriateness of a tip by whether she would have been satisfied with it back when her parents were paying her rent, and she was bartending for shoes. As a bartender with a fondness for designer footwear, her estimates ran to the high side. She opened the taxi door to find the driver had positioned her directly in front of one of the larger puddles.

"Fuck, dude. Are you kidding me? Pull up a little."

"Sorry, miss. I can't stop in a crosswalk. I'm not supposed to stop here either. Hurry up and get out before I get a ticket."

Experience told her the driver was not going to budge, and so, having no other choice, she placed a stiletto down into the disgusting mess, cursing the cab driver who had — she was sure — purposely chosen this spot for her to disembark in payment for some cultural slight of which she wasn't even remotely aware.

Carolyn flexed her ankles and rose from the seat of the cab with silver-tipped heels down and the front of both feet pointed straight out in the air, hovering five inches above the shallow lake of dog pee. She proceeded in that peculiar duck walk common to New York women for whom shoes consume a good portion of their disposable income and sailed across the sea of urine like a glamorous stilt-walker, crimson soles dry and face composed, much as Jesus might have strolled across the Sea of Galilee had he possessed a pair of five-inch, ankle-strap Louboutins.

Landing safely on dry ground and relaxing her ankles into their more usual downward slanted position, Carolyn strode purposefully to the door of Bubby's, deeply inhaling the Tribeca air, its unpleasant odors tinged ever so slightly with the nearby sea air and the even nearer-by aroma of celebrity. She threw open the door and the smells of the city locked into nasal combat with the welcoming scents of Bubby's: pies, waffles, and best of all, grits. Carolyn could pick out the warm, comforting, buttery smell of grits from all the other warm, comforting, buttery smells that wafted out of the restaurant. By the time the door closed, the smell of dog piss was but a distant memory. Bubby's smelled like grits and fame. Two of Carolyn's favorites.

"Can I get my usual table by the window, Sonia?" Carolyn asked the hostess, having read her name tag as she approached her. "And bring us the usual. Grits, eggs, bacon, pancakes, the works. For two. My business partner will be joining me today."

The hostess started to inform Carolyn that she was a hostess and not a waitress. She would seat her when she was good and damned ready, and she didn't know her from Adam's housecat, so she could forget this "usual" bullshit, but it wasn't worth the agita. She rolled her eyes and let it go. Let the bitch seat herself. One less thing to do. Besides, Trust Fund PAs (as the hostess had incorrectly pegged Carolyn) sometimes became producers, and who knows, if she took a little shit from the rude girl, maybe the rude girl would read her screenplay.

Carolyn knew the woman didn't recognize her. How could she? Carolyn could only afford to eat breakfast at Bubby's a couple of times a month. But the dark, handsome piece of tasty Eurotrash in Gucci shades and Prada kicks she had spotted at the front table didn't know that, and Carolyn was playing to him just now.

Turning on her best catwalk strut for the stubbly-faced stranger, Carolyn glided to the table she had selected as her usual one — crossing one leg far across the centerline of her body and placing her high-heel-shod foot down in front of the other leg with each long stride, a motion designed to initiate maximum hip sway from hips that were virtually nonexistent. It was an eye-catching move for a stick-straight model. For Carolyn, who, though slim, was quite shapely, it was riveting. The hostess's annoyance with Carolyn turned to envy. If she could walk like that in those shoes, she mused, she might be handing out headshots instead of screenplays.

Carolyn slid into a chair, prepared to almost, but not quite, make eye contact with her prey, carefully locking her crimson lips into the impenetrable pout of the genetic mutants she emulated so well. At that exact moment, her business partner slid into the seat opposite her and blocked her view of the handsome European.

"It's a little early in the morning to be stalking Eurotrash, isn't it?" Robby asked her, leaning across the table and ostentatiously kissing the faintly Romeo Gigli-scented air beside each of Carolyn's cheeks.

"Damn it, Robby. Where the fuck did you come from? You ruined my dismount. And why the fuck are you kissing me? Now he's going to think we're an item."

"You think? It's just an air kiss." Robby began to turn in his seat.

"Don't look!" Carolyn whisper-shrieked.

Robby continued to turn until he met eyes with the tall, dark European — his knockoff Gucci shades locking mirrors with the other man's genuine Gucci shades — and then shook out his shaggy brown hair, long silver streaks waving all the way from his temples to his shoulders. He then twirled one of the striking white streaks around his index finger, never breaking Gucci-clad eye contact, before he smiled slightly and turned back around.

"What in the actual fuck was that?" asked Carolyn, dazed, if not dazzled, by the performance.

"Well, now he knows we're not together, and he's got to decide which one of us he's going to hit on if he indeed plans to hit on either of us."

"But you're not gay."

"An observation that is irrelevant to this exercise. If you do begin going out with that slick, arrogant asshole, and he grows distant— as he inevitably will— and you're worrying yourself to death trying to figure out what the fuck the problem is— as you inevitably will— you can scratch his being secretly gay from the list of possible reasons for your misery, because, well, if he chooses you over me, he's definitely not gay."

Carolyn's studied pout broke, and she laughed out loud. "You're a nut. What are you going to do if he asks you out?"

"I sincerely doubt that will happen, Carolyn. He's not the going-out type. Though I wouldn't be surprised if he tries to do me in the men's room. I also won't be surprised if you end up with him, and by 'end up with him,' I mean having sweaty sex on the floor of your apartment. But he's not taking you out in public any more than he would me."

"Fuck you, asshole." Carolyn was drawn to men who were more into fucking her than dating her, and Robbie knew it as well as she did. He actually knew it better than she did, and it annoyed the crap out of her. When Robby had been friend-zoned by Carolyn immediately upon their meeting six years before, he had not been surprised. Women of her striking beauty were seldom interested in an average-looking guy like himself—his hair was his best feature and what woman wants a man with better hair than she has—but more than their disparity on the one to ten appearance meter, Carolyn was one of those beautiful women who demanded a large degree of assholery from her paramours, far more than Robby was capable of providing, and thus they had settled into the comfortable role of friends whose partnership extended only to matters of business.

"Why can't you get a menu in this clipjoint? It's Sunday morning, and there's hardly anybody here, except for smoldering Gucci/Prada over there," Robbie said, as he turned once again in his seat, this time in search of their waitress.

"No problem. I've already ordered."

"How did you already order? Your ass hadn't hit your chair when I walked in."

"Well, I have. Grits are on the way."

"Fuck, no. It's bad enough we have to work on Sunday. And it's bad enough you insist on eating at Bubba's, but there is no way in hell I'm eating those ridiculous goddamned grits again."

"You're right. It's bad enough we have to work on Sunday. But we have a meeting with a potential Italian sales rep tomorrow morning, and we are going to nail it if it takes us all day to prep."

"I see that nailing Europeans is going to be a running theme for the day's activities."

"Cute. But you know as well as I do that our one Paris account moves more product than any five US doors put together. They get us over there. Tomorrow is our big chance to increase our European profile, and we won't get another one before we run out of money and have to shut this bitch down."

"Okay."

"There is no way I am going back to bartending. And Barneys is closed, so you can't go back to making cappuccinos for movie stars. So eat up. It's going to be a long day. And seriously, how can you be in TriBeCa on Sunday morning and not eat grits at Bubby's? Is that even possible?"

"Very possible," Robby sighed, as he slumped down in his seat, puzzled again for the millionth time as to why his business partner was so enamored of grits. Carolyn was a born-and-bred Connecticut girl who disguised the DAR pageboy of her people with a bright red SoHo salon dye job and bangs of defiance, a not entirely successful obliteration of her preppy background. How in the world did a girl like that even know what grits were?

"Stop looking so forlorn. You don't have to eat your grits if you don't want to. I just don't understand how you can pass them up when we're right here. Bubby's is the only place I know of in Manhattan that serves grits."

"Which puts Bubba's at the bottom of the list of places I want to eat."

"It's Bubby's. Not Bubba's. Why do you always get that wrong?"

"Trust me, I haven't gotten anything wrong. It's Bubba's."

"Okay, so you're from the South, and you know all about bubbas. That makes it all the more confusing to me why you don't like grits. They should bring you nostalgic comfort if nothing else."

"Grits are for poor people."

"That's ridiculous. Do you see any poor people in here? This is TriBeCa, land of the fuck-you rich. Everybody in this diner could buy and sell your average Upper East Sider before lunch, and most of them have their hungover faces slumped over in a plate full of grits."

"We're poor."

"No, we're broke. There's a big difference. But you told me you grew up poor, so why don't you eat grits?"

"I did grow up poor. But I'm town poor. Not country poor. There's a big difference."

"What's the difference?"

"People who are town poor don't eat grits. And we don't have mean-ass yard chickens hiding out under our houses while they wait to become Sunday dinners. And our sandwiches are made with store-bought Wonder bread, not leftover biscuits. But mainly, we don't eat possums or squirrels. Or grits."

"Quite the caste system you had there in North Carolina."

"Said the girl from Farmington, Connecticut, home of Miss Warner's Finishing School for Young Ladies of Refinement and Sizeable Trust Funds."

"Oh, Jesus. How many times do I have to tell you that girls who live in Farmington don't go to Miss Warner's? It's a freaking boarding school.

Those privileged hussies fly in on their goddamned broomsticks from Palm Beach or the Upper East Side or Gstaad or wherever the fuck they are spawned."

"But don't you hang with them at dances or cotillions or whatever shit you do in Connecticut?"

"Robby, we were fucking townies."

"You were not a fucking townie. Your father was an insurance executive, and he built a yacht in your garage after he enlarged the garage so it would hold the yacht he was about to build."

"It wasn't a yacht. It was a trimaran sailboat."

"Did it have a cabin?"

"Of course."

"Then it was a yacht."

"Well, we weren't rich. We were comfortable. Rich people don't build yachts in their garages."

"Oh, comfortable, were you? Said every rich person ever who didn't want to cop to being rich. I'm sure all the Van Rensselaer and Rockefeller girls at Miss Warner's were clamoring to come over to your house and check out the progress on Daddy's yacht."

"Those bitches didn't know we existed. Except maybe when one of them needed some help throwing a baby in a dumpster."

"What?"

"Oh, yeah. When I was in high school —public high school, mind you — they found a dead baby, a newborn still covered in birthing goo, in a dumpster. Turns out, one of those Miss Warner cunts had a baby in her dorm room and tossed it in the dumpster. Can you believe that? It's one thing if you're homeless and hungry or a freaked-out 12-year old, but that bitch could have jumped on Daddy's private jet and flown to Switzerland for an abortion or an adoption. If she caught a ride with Mummy going over for some sheep-hormone injections, no one would have even noticed she was missing. They could have probably gone to the same freakin' all-purpose rich-bitch clinic."

Robby was stunned. Carolyn looked like the WASPiest of WASPs, but she was, in fact, a good Catholic girl, and more religious than she usually let on. That she considered an abortion preferable to throwing a live baby into a dumpster surprised him. More than a little.

"I never heard about that. I think I would have heard about that."

Carolyn gave Robby her wise-in-the-ways-of-the-world look and its matching world-weary sigh, as she shook her head and ever so slightly rolled her eyes.

"Those girls don't make the news. They don't go to jail. They don't get arrested. They don't get a damned jaywalking ticket if they fuck a Yale man in the middle of the town square against the light."

"Must make Farmington an interesting place to live."

"Tell me about it."

"So you think it's okay for a freaked-out 12-year-old or a starving, homeless woman to have an abortion?"

"Sure I do. Don't you?"

"I think every woman has the right to choose what goes on inside her body. But I'm not religious. I don't have an imaginary friend telling me he knows what's best for everybody else."

"Well, even practicing Catholics find themselves in a tight spot from time to time. You do know, don't you, that the anti-abortion bitches get as many abortions as women who are pro-choice?"

"Yeah, I know that. It's never made any sense to me."

"It doesn't, until what you believe comes into direct conflict with what you need."

"Have you ever had to make that choice?"

"That is an unacceptable question. It's none of your damn business if I've ever seen the inside of an abortion clinic."

"I'm sorry. I have."

"You have what?"

"I've seen the inside of an abortion clinic. Or at least the waiting room."

"What?"

"Well, as it turns out, vaginal foam is not all that effective as a means of birth control."

"Jesus, that stuff is nasty."

"You're telling me. But nasty would have been okay if the damn shit worked. But it didn't."

"Fuck."

"You got it. That's exactly why I had occasion to be at Park Med cooling my heels in the waiting room while my ex-girlfriend took care of business in the back. She was terrified. So was I, to be honest."

"I'm impressed that you went with her."

"Well, I couldn't send her by herself to face a gantlet of rabid assholes calling her a slut and waving bloody pictures at her. But the clinic was on the 26th floor of a Park Avenue office building so, thankfully, she was spared that. We mixed in with the other people coming and going from the building and didn't have to deal with any nutballs."

"Yet one more reason to live in New York. It must be awful for those poor girls living out in flyover country. So if you're such a gent, did you pay for the procedure while you were there?"

"I never claimed to be a gentleman."

"So you didn't pay for the abortion. Did you at least go Dutch?"

"Of course I paid for it. It was the least I could do. Well, that and be there with her."

"You're right, it was the least you could do. But I guess it was also the most you could do."

Their waitress approached the table, weighed down with platters of pancakes and bacon and eggs and two big portions of grits slathered in melting butter.

"I still don't like grits. They sound like dirt," Robby said as he smoothed his napkin over his left knee.

"Yum," said Carolyn, surveying with great happiness the bounty which Robby thought looked identical to the country breakfasts his Great-Mammy — she of the aggressive yard chickens lurking under her rickety old house — cooked up every day of her life on her wood stove. His displeasure at the grits on the table was mitigated somewhat by the thought that Great-Mammy would surely faint if she saw the check that would be placed on their table in a few minutes. Great-Mammy had been country poor. She had died without ever having a toilet inside her house, but she had lived to see some of her grandchildren move into town and climb up the ladder to town poor. She would never have believed in a million years that one of her great-grandchildren would someday move to New York City and pay eight dollars for a spoonful of grits he didn't want.

Carolyn dug into her grits with lusty abandon, and Robby eyed the nasty mess, determined to take at least a bite or two because he was only two generations removed from country poor and his people did not waste food. As Robby stared at his plate, steeling himself to dig into the unappetizing goo, a shadow fell across the table.

Robby and Carolyn both looked up and saw it was the handsome European from the front table. Carolyn lunged for her napkin and began furiously blotting butter from the corners of her crimson lips.

"I see you both have the polenta. It's delizioso, is it not?"

"Si, delizioso," agreed Carolyn.

"We're not having polenta. We've got grits," said Robby.

"But it is the same thing, no?"

"I suppose it is," said Carolyn.

"Polenta certainly sounds better," said Robby.

"When I was a child in Napoli, my Nonna would make us a huge pot of polenta when there was nothing else to eat. It still gives me, as you Americans say, the warm fuzzies."

Carolyn gave Robby a superior smirk.

"I've never been to New York in August before. It is very quiet."

"Especially on the weekend," agreed Carolyn. "Most everyone has escaped to the beach. We have work to do, or we'd be at my beach house in Sag Harbor."

Robby shifted his gaze from their guest to Carolyn, a quizzical look on his face. This was the first he had heard of Carolyn's alleged beach house in Sag Harbor. "I thought your family summered in Old Saybrook."

"We do, but it's about time I flew the nest, so I'm leasing a cottage in Sag Harbor for the summer."

"Oh, then perhaps you'll invite me for the weekend sometime," said Robby. "Maybe next weekend. Maybe you'll invite us both." He gestured toward the handsome stranger.

"Oh, no," said the man. "Unfortunately, I must return to Italia before the weekend returns."

"Unfortunately," said Carolyn, with a sigh conveying both relief and regret.

"My name is Giancarlo," said the man.

"I'm Carolyn, and this is Robby."

Giancarlo reached into his pocket and pulled out a card. Carolyn reached out to take the card, as Giancarlo turned to offer it to Robby. "I am staying at the Mercer Hotel, Robby. My room number is on the back. But you will probably find me in the lobby bar this evening. Perhaps you could join me there."

"Perhaps," replied Robby.

"I like your hair. I love Elsa Lanchester."

Robby once again reached for one of the long silver streaks growing from his temples, and unconsciously began to twirl it.

"You're saying I look like the Bride of Frankenstein?"

"No, you look like her hot brother."

"That's sweet, Giancarlo. And I like that Marcello Mastroianni vibe you've got going. It's very '8½'." Robby took the card and laid it on the table in front of him.

"I see we both like the cinema. We'll have lots to talk about this evening. Ciao," said Giancarlo, before turning and walking out of Bubby's.

"What in the actual fuck was that?" asked Carolyn for the second time in twenty minutes. "Did he say you looked like Frankenstein while he was putting the moves on you? And besides, you're not gay," she added, perplexed.

"I never said that. You just assumed."

"What about the girl at Park Med?"

"What about her?" Robby shrugged. "Life is a banquet, and most poor suckers are starving to death, as Auntie Mame used to say. And speaking of banquets, this polenta is delizioso."

Carolyn burst out into peals of laughter, and Robby looked up from his plate to see that she had picked up Giancarlo's card.

"What's so funny?"

"I suggest you be on your A-game tonight. And don't keep Giancarlo up too late. We have a meeting with him at nine in the morning, when Mr. Smoldering Gucci-Prada is going to decide if our business sinks or swims. I think I'll go to the office now."

"But you've barely touched your breakfast."

"I've suddenly lost my appetite. And when you get to the office, I would prefer we never speak of this again."

Carolyn leaned across the table, air-kissed both of Robby's cheeks before standing up and heading for the door, model strut fully engaged, all eyes upon her once again. When she reached the front door, she turned back to Robby and stage-whispered, "Mangia, darling. No pun intended," before heading out into the dog-piss-infused TriBeCa morning.

Katie Bowers

Sacral

My hips are so heavy. At night they ache;
they groan, as if to signal that rain is coming

They say:
*This is for the burden of those who
have laid on and have pressed against,
for those who loved you or used you
or missed you before you left or
those who didn't understand their own
weight.*

*This is for the first pregnancy,
the joints and ligaments loosening
a few week's worth of centimeters,
and for the second pregnancy,
where the same joints, the same ligaments,
were allowed to unravel like a spool
of thread.*

*This is for all the miles you choose
to run alone, all the bricks you carry,
all the books you rest against your hip,
all the ways you bend and stretch and
pose and stand alone.*

They ask:
*Do you remember how your husband would
wake up at two in the morning (walk to the
other side of the bed) gently take your hands
and pull you out of bed (the weight of his child
pressing against your bladder) because your hips
hurt too much for you to get up on your own?*

*Do you remember how good it felt to
crouch low, to let the grief be carried
on more than just yourself?*

They know.

Katie Bowers

Sixteen Plus Sixteen is Thirty-Two
(or Fifteen Plus Fifteen is Thirty?)

i lost my virginity at sixteen
(or maybe fifteen?)[1]

it has been half my life
(or maybe more?)[2]

and i have had sex with three
(or was it five?)
(or was it twenty?)
people[3]

but believing it to be three (is it five or is it twenty?)[4]
my mother would have called me
one of the following adjectives:
a whore, a real slut, a skank
(none of the above)?[5]

but who gives a fuck
about that anymore

---

1. *i truly do not remember*
2. *this is contingent upon the first stanza*
3. *i know how many but it doesn't matter*
4. *it was three, she thought it was three*
5. *whore*

Terry Barr

Best Friends

Sam rings the doorbell promptly at eight. He's here to watch the Yankees' playoff game. When I open the door, he's holding a six-pack of Beck's.

"I can drink beer," he says, "just not hard liquor."

Because everyone knows that if you've already had to dry out twice, just a few beers won't cause any more damage.

It's his life, and I'm too caught in grief to try to talk logic to an alcoholic. He and his wife split up a year earlier, a shock, given who and how they were. Newly married, they served in Teach for America together. They were, Sam used to say, "best friends."

And mutual friends with us. Parents, like us. Rock solid, we thought, or at least I did.

I have seen Sam drunk only once, when the four of us ate together at a place called The Owl. That night, I sat down first and Sam sat on the same side of our table with me. I'm not sure what he was thinking, or how many "beers" he had already consumed. He has one of those voices, a "Gomer Pyle" nasal twang, only northern. Sam is from Chicago, and when his college football team was beating mine that same year, he kept calling me to crow. If, that is, a crow could talk after "a beer or two" in a northern nasal twang.

That night at The Owl he kept whispering (he thought) to me. Things about the food, the hipster atmosphere, his wife. I kept looking at mine, and she at me. She didn't smile. The evening ran on, but the four of us never went out again.

I understand now why his wife did what she did, even though I know it hurt them both.

"You have to understand," my wife said. "Everyone has a story. And she's my friend, but still, I keep a distance."

And now, the distance between him and me on this couch is

unsettling as we watch a game that in previous years I would have been crazed or impassioned or obnoxious about. Yes, I get that way, too, especially about sports, especially when it doesn't matter.

What does matter is that my best friend died exactly a year ago, and my mother died four months ago, and my cat disappeared two months ago, and tomorrow we're going back to Alabama to clear out my mother's house, to ready it for sale. And so I don't really give a fuck about the Yankees tonight, but that's the basis of my relationship with Sam. We're Yankees' fans, and Aaron Judge has just come on the scene, and something like tonight is supposed to distract me from whatever I will have to do tomorrow and all that I have been doing these last months.

Like executing my best friend's will.

Like wondering where we'll store my mother's antique furniture.

Like fighting the urge to leave this place, a fight Sam's ex-wife, a spiritual mystic, helped me wage.

And now two beers in (in addition to whatever he had consumed before coming over), Sam is leaning in to me and asking about our mutual friend Jerry who Sam says has lost it:

"I mean, Terry, what's the matter with him? Everyone in his office talks about him. I heard one woman ask, 'What's his problem…who does he think he is?' and then she shook her head like he was poison!"

I have no answers and don't even understand the questions. Or rather, I don't understand why this man is asking such questions of me? Like I'll say something to Jerry? Like Sam and I are in agreement?

Like we're good friends in this together?

***

My best friend, who was diagnosed with and died from lung cancer all in the span of October 2017, asked me to be his estate executor long before he knew he was dying or even sick.

"Sure I will," I said. "Of course!"

Then I forgot all about the request, as I think I was supposed to. In a fit of spiritual magic, I didn't think it would ever happen. Nor did I know—and why would I?—that when you execute someone's will, you are legally allowed to take a percentage of the estate for yourself. Something like 6%. A day after his death and still before complete reality had kicked in, my best friend's brother urged me to take the money:

"After you spend eighteen months sorting through this, you'll want it," he said. "You'll believe you earned it."

The only thing he got wrong was that it took twenty-eight months to sort out the will, and that was with everyone's being friendly about how death gets divided.

At the start, I didn't want the money, and then, when it got to the end, I did. But I still don't think I "earned it."

Who can be the judge of such things, the residue of such friendships?

Back in the world of Yankee baseball, Judge homered, I think, and the Yankees won, only to get bounced from the playoffs a few nights later. So it goes with America's past time, and a game that could theoretically last forever. Sam drank three beers and left the rest for me. Was this a kind gesture of how we were with each other, or his particular form of discipline?

Before he left that night, though, he asked about my best friend and how I was coping with my grief.

"He was your bestie!"

It was one of those sobering statements, and I still appreciate that somewhere in him, he understood. Which was, I think now, another way of wishing that he could experience what my best friend and I had together. Experience it once again, maybe, with someone new, now that he was single.

Now that he was all alone and lonely in his midnight rambling hour.

***

After my best friend died, and while grief still held me tightly, my brother-in-law suggested,

"Maybe I could be your best friend now."

How could I tell him? Best friends aren't selected from a menu, via a direct request, or really by any choice. Sometimes a best friend happens to you because you both love Lou Reed, or your dogs. Or because you show up to the same chapter meeting of Amnesty International on the same first night. You're looking for human rights, and to be closer to something, perhaps to someone. A certain kind of person whose soul isn't for borrowing, or for sale.

"No, I don't think so" my grief said.

We were sitting outside at a Starbucks in the middle of a Friday afternoon. He paid for our cappuccinos and then we drove away in our separate cars.

It pays to be an executor, but does it pay to turn down someone who asks to be an intimate?

***

After the game I watch Sam drive away. He's offered to look after our dog while we're in Alabama, but I don't want someone who drinks just a few beers and believes they won't do him any harm to care for my precious pal. So, I tell him we have it covered, which we do.

Did he mean it? Could he have done it? Was that a friendly, caring gesture? Should I have given him hope?

I watch him do a 360 in front of my house, and the last thing I see just under his tail lights as he roars away is his bumper sticker:

"Keith Richards Is My Spirit Animal."

***

The last time I see Sam is at his ex-wife's mother's funeral. He gets up, and in a shaky voice, he speaks of how much he loved his ex-mother-in-law—how well she always treated him and accepted him. How she didn't let divorce stop her from assuring him of her love.

Terry Barr **67**

Should we have believed that? How would we ever know? I didn't know the woman myself, nor could I guess what his ex-wife had revealed to her. About Sam, about herself.

Before he got up to speak, Sam found me and hugged me and asked if I'd like to take a road trip with him that coming summer to Cooperstown—to see Derek Jeter be inducted into the Hall of Fame.

"Man, I don't think so," I say. "We'll be visiting our daughter in the mountains during July." And maybe that's what we'll really be doing.

"Ok, I understand," he says, and then he moves on to other friends. Only one of his two daughters attends the event, because when a family breaks, nothing is ever even again.

And as he hugged me, I noticed that aroma, the one many alcoholics can never fully hide or truly shed.

This was the week before the Coronavirus hit.

So I could have put Sam off and not have lied about the coming summer.

But maybe what I did was better, a clearer response, even though in that moment, I still saw too many shadows of grief that I literally staggered back to my seat. Anyway, I wouldn't have driven with him to Cooperstown or anywhere else. Not even before I knew these things about him—the things maybe a friend would have, should have, known so much earlier. We've just never been that close, though for a time, I think we tried.

I haven't seen him since that funeral setting, even though Sam lives less than a mile from me, still alone, I suppose, in a reconditioned apartment complex. I pass by his place frequently, but I never pause. His apartment is usually dark anyway.

He still drives the same car, too, and it's usually parked in the same space out front. And though it's dented now in significant ways, its rear bumper still claims that Keith Richards is his spirit animal.

Katie Bowers

Conversations

On Thursday evenings my husband turns to me,
he asks, *Do you even like me?*

I shrug and roll my eyes while tucking in on my side.
Tired from the dark things that have spun webs in my brain
all day, all the week, all my life.

His hand still finds its way to me in his sleep.
Do you even like me? The weight of his palm in mine.

On crisp Saturday mornings, my husband turns to me,
and I say, *Your hands write poetry along my hip
bones, and when you are turned towards the morning
light, the sight of your freckled shoulders, bared
to me, I know your forehead is smoothed of its worried,
contemplative wrinkles, and, of course, I like you.*

How could I not, when the wrinkles have deepened,
the freckles have grown, the hair has grayed, the
energy has waned, and yet, his hand still finds its
way to me as he dreams.

Kathie Collins

This Is the Work of the Dream

You know how stubborn I can be—unwilling to play the fool
for anyone's love. But the dream gives me a chance to plead

my case. Beg you to stay. The dream doesn't know you already
left. For her, first. Then forever. The dream has no philosophy or religion.

It sits on the side of my heart, which in its old age begins to flutter—
silvered wings warming up for that final migration.

The dream doesn't care where you are. No need for a map
to find you. It simply hoists time's curtain, puts us on stage together

to work out the toughest scene. And my dumb hard heart—
so focused on tapping its forward march, utterly duped by its refusal

of pain—suddenly discovers the dream's terrible mercy: the dream
is the knife. It splits its leathered rind, peels away pith, digs

through decades of hidden longing toward the center.
To uncover an astonishing cache of seeds.

Andrew DeVoy

Sweeteners, Why We Use Them

The Eritrean's name was Eyob. He pulled out an English Bible and flipped to his transliteration: Job. I told him I understood and offered him a pastry, but between foosball shots on goal and terribly broken phrases in a third language, Eyob informed me that he was vegan until May. I ate the pastry. We took a break from foosball and Eyob consented to a coffee. "No cream, just black. Vegan, remember?" He tapped at his chest, as if he was reminding me of his name.

Eyob explained to me that every year his people fast from all animal products for forty days leading up to Easter. "Not even chicken! No animal, not any food from animal!" His wide open, cataract-affected eyes matched the urgency of his white teeth as he spoke. It was important that I caught on. It was important that I should know not to serve him half-and-half and how devoutly orthodox he was. I nodded and slid a mug of black coffee across the table. He held four sugar packets, already torn open, between his thumb and index finger. I couldn't help the grin that broke across my face. Eyob was vibrating; he was already so full of sugar and caffeine. For all I knew, he had been at the coffee shop since they opened.

That was nearly all there was to do for the refugees in Ittigen. They could spend the day in a concrete bunker-turned-housing-bay, under a parking lot in an industrial section of the city. They could misunderstand most of an argument with immigration officials at the local office. Or, they could sit at a coffee shop and hope the Swiss locals might teach them German, French, English, anything of value. The sugar packets writhed like mice in his shaking hand as he dumped them into his coffee, a huge smile on his small round head.

When I was very young, I found two small brown dropper bottles in my father's refrigerator door. Stevia, from before I was born. For a decade or so, the bottles sat and spread their stickiness down themselves, which finally cemented them to the shelf. I happened upon them fossilized in the fridge the same way archeologists sometimes find whole pots of the water of youth in the tombs of men-once-gods. Mercury, arsenic, gold, sugar and mint to taste, suspended in an eternal tonic, in the dark. Untouched and getting stickier by the century.

The bottles were from my mother, who was always hopping on health kicks. It was a new word for her to learn—to ask fellow Californians whether they knew the benefits, or if they knew where to find it. Some of her health kicks wouldn't last more than a month. She must have discovered stevia shortly before she left.

I laughed with Eyob about the four sugars in his coffee, and asked him if he'd ever heard of stevia. He said he hadn't, and I told him he should never try it—that the taste wasn't worth whatever calorie-free benefits it offered. "Calorie-free?" He didn't understand. I tried to explain that many westerners preferred to eat food that made them thinner. "Like Christians fast?" He asked. There was a depth in Eyob's eyes, cloudy as they were. They sought a connection from me that I couldn't match. It felt violative to spend time explaining that the only thing so many Europeans and Americans were devout about—the only god they served—was the maintenance of self-image. "No, not the same as fasting," I sighed, frowning to communicate a breakdown in my language; that, he understood.

Hoping to be clearer and use images Eyob would understand, I pivoted. This was all good English practice for him, after all. I told him there's a sugar beet processing plant in my hometown. How I grew up driving past huge white dunes of beet waste, believing the waste was in fact all the sugar they made. How I imagined standing at the top of the sugar dune in a heroic pose and then throwing myself down the hill, somersaulting so many times I'd look like a candied mango slice at the bottom. He fired out a laugh and with two wiry arms he gestured pouring a mountain of invisible sugar into his vegan black coffee. We cackled together, bouncing up and down in our plastic chairs. Understanding each other's eyes and bodies more than we ever could with our words. "This make good coffee," he said, and I nodded in agreement, finishing my mug. Eyob volunteered to refill our coffees, making mine like he took his: vegan, black, so much sugar.

"How old are you?" I asked. He looked grandfatherly in the face, though his eyes were brightening as we talked. "I am fifty-seven. Old grandpa, huh?"

"No, that's my dad's age." I told Eyob I could be his son, not his grandson. He pulled up a folder of pictures on a smartphone and swiped through a dozen low quality shots of his family. Some were smiling, others maintained a kind of stoic face you don't see much in the West anymore. "Your family is beautiful," what else could I say. Then, Eyob stopped on a different photo. A handful of men posing on the crest of a yellow sand dune, all dressed in fatigues, AK-47s and MP5s slung around wiry limbs. Eyob took a sip from the fresh mug. His wide, cataract-affected eyes matched the openness of his toothy smile. "I fight for my people back there. Now I am here, no home. No more fighting, no more guns. I leave them in Eritrea when I leave."

Greg Nelson

Cradled in My Arms in the Wee Hours

my son's cry could turn to gold
all the cold distances in the world

without a fever or a tummy ache
he's holding nothing back

yesterday on the slide
he beamed like a second sun

no worries
I'll rock you till
the sandman returns

as if inside the din he can hear me
or would care if he could

eyes screwed shut he's hard at work
purging a thorn too deep

if he pines for his mother
she's days away

if he pines for one roof over
two voices comingling in one wave
before it broke I've cried too

a friend said I needn't worry
about Isaiah he's so young
he won't remember any of this

still I fear his heart won't forget
his first world

and too soon he's learning
forever comes to an end

    his cry has crested
and started to soften

brother to brother we sway together
balanced on roots deeper than night

Greg Nelson 75

Anya Russian

Blink

It is the beaming moon I admire tonight, sure as a weathered coin long lodged in a pocket. It is the same moon that oversees the violence of its miniatures below. I want to call it lust. The plenitude, that is. Or the greed of the heron pleating the sky with its singular flight. There are few shelters so luminous, steady beyond our tending. I cannot believe in the man or a woman beneath such elation. I cannot comprehend the divergent course elation takes. How there are shards that glimmer alongside the bougainvillea. How quickly the water exonerates a blade. There is no detour—though it seems otherwise. Nothing to capsize, no cursor to move elsewhere. I find it hard to blink sometimes. Preferring, or fortunate, to know the starkest blights from a relative distance—one of beauty's stowaways—or not so old yet to concede the crimson turns to rust. But perhaps that is savage too. While so many gazes pummeled under so much dark, blindly beam back the only light left for us.

Quentin Steadman

Cold Blooded

The kid showed up again. A boy - seven, maybe eight - with a red shirt and blue pocket stitched on the side. He wore it every day for the past week. Robbie and I were parked in the usual spot: across the street from the music store we planned to rob. To our left, just beyond a strip of sidewalk, the optometrist I visited a few times started filling with people. Some of them had kids they ushered in with a hand while holding the door open. I never bought anything there, nor did I get a checkup. Couldn't afford that, not out of pocket. But whenever I accidentally bent the frames of the glasses I do own, they'd let me come in and fix them for free.   I didn't even know there was a music store a block over. Why was this kid alone?

Robbie reclined in the driver's seat watching videos on his phone. I crinkled the edge of my notebook filled with alternate names for people - Sad Sam, Most-likely Martha, Jumpsuit Janice, Fred Flannel - clocking in and out every day at the store I watched like a hawk; or I assumed they did, considering how often they showed up and the intervals of their arrival and departure (which I marked in a different color pen because I never robbed anyone before and wanted to play it safe). Every day - except Sunday - one of them parked in the parking lot the music store shared with the strip of businesses and walked over to unlock the place at 11 in the morning.

Before they did, I'd occasionally look through my binoculars and find the kid returning for another day of no one accompanying him. Down the sidewalk he wandered, alone, stopping several feet away from the music store to plop himself down on the very edge of a yard belonging to the last house, right before grass gave way to asphalt. He'd sit there and stare out in the street. Sometimes he'd tear up handfuls of grass. When one of the employees closed shop at eight he'd still be there, watching the streets and tearing grass.

"Jumpsuit Janice, 10:55," I said with a quick glance towards the parking lot where a woman sauntered from the door of a massive silver truck and down the sidewalk in a pair of vanilla thigh-highs and a denim one-piece. When she unlocked the door with a large set of keys pulled from her purse, I noticed the back of her outfit spelled out 'bubblegum' in diamonds. She disappeared inside, flipping the *closed* sign to *open* with a flick of her wrist.

Robbie only grunted at my announcement, continuing to watch the screen he held in his palms. He was dead set on this plan of his. Robbie told me he'd been practicing his imitation all week. He'd been listening to one of the interviews our target conducted with a local radio station about his collection of famous instruments.

"Do you think it'll be Sam or Fred?" I asked, just to give myself something to do besides watching the kid. Did his parents know where he was at? What if he got kidnapped?

"Dunno." Robbie scratched his nose. I caught tiny voices from the speakers. Their pitch was raised, talking excitedly between laughter. Someone asked the other, What was it like to own Eddie Hazel's Stratocaster?

Like a hot potato, haha! one of the voices boomed. It was Giacometti, our man, the owner of the music store. He continued shouting, Out of my hands before the end of the day, haha!

"Like a hot potato..." Robbie repeated each word slowly, murmuring their syllables again and again. He closed his eyes, craning his neck towards the car's roof. "Po-ta-to. PUH-ta-to..."

What if this kid's parents were dead? Or dying. Did he know to call 9-1-1? I wondered if he could speak and felt my heart quicken at the idea of him not being able to tell someone about his parents being dead - or dying. I moved to my seatbelt's buckle and pressed lightly on the red button. That had to be it. I'll ask him. I'd walk over and say, Hello, you don't know me but you can tell me if you parents are hurt. Are they hurt? Here, write it down. That's when I'd hand him my notebook and he'd finally be able to tell someone instead of sitting all alone on some random street with no supervision.

I paused. What if he lived there? I brought up my binoculars and peered into them. The house was a sky blue painted cottage, with a rusty Plymouth sleeping in the driveway. Cracks along the concrete gave way to unruly weeds which grew along the car's tires as if it hadn't been driven in a while. A window was boarded up with planks of wood. Since we started the stakeout, I couldn't recall ever seeing someone step outside or peek through the window curtain. If the little boy lived there he'd go and check-in every now and then so his parent's knew what he was up to, even if it was sitting in the yard and making bald spots amongst the grass. I could go over and tell him that. Walk up to him and say, Hello, you don't know me, but it's important that you tell your parents where you are and what you are doing. Did you know that? He might be surprised - aren't kids always surprised at something - but he'd be thankful, that I know for sure. I should do it.

Robbie sat up. He touched my shoulder. "Listen to this." I turned to face him as he worked his jaw in quick circles, taking small breaths and licking his lips. He looked like a maniac.

"Like a hot potato!"

"Emphasize the *hot*," I told him. Settling back in my seat. I saw that the boy was still pulling up grass and tossing it over his sneakers. He stared at the ground. His hair looked like an overgrown bowl cut someone forgot to tend to. No one should just let their child loose - at least this young - for nine hours at a time without once checking up on them or making them check-in at home every now and then. The weather had been ideal for the past week but this kid hadn't eaten anything or had a bit to drink the entire time I watched him. I kept peeking glances between the glass doors of the music shop and him.

Maybe I should ask Robbie to call this whole thing off. Another time. But I knew he'd be upset and he'd talk about the deal we made and how easy this was all going to be. Perfect, he told me over and over. Giacometti liked to visit his shop, liked to remind himself of what he owned. This time, he managed to get his hands on a vintage 1973 Rickenbacker bass guitar, model 4001. White with black binding and a smooth rosewood fretboard. Robbie said this one, near its tuning pegs, had seven individual knicks in the wood. Quick, vertical slashes with a pocket knife or something similar. Each one represented an album Rick James recorded, using this guitar for most of his early to mid-career tracks.

When Robbie told me it was Rick James' guitar, I didn't believe it. Who's Rick James? He played guitar? Yes, Robbie said, look. He opened the glove compartment in his car and CDs started spilling out. Grabbing one, Robbie held it up and pointed to the front cover. Rick was there, holding the guitar. They made it just for him, Robbie pressed, excitement clear in his words. His was custom, man. Rick James, man.

And he just had this thing out on the floor, I asked Robbie.

Yea, yea, Robbie said. In the middle. It's got its own pedestal.

Robbie promised he'd have it sold in three days. Apparently, he knew a guy in Atlanta and already had a deal lined up and we were to go there immediately after stealing the guitar. We were going to split the earnings down the middle. I didn't have any money, nor did I have a job. My mail consisted of bills from Virginia and Pennsylvania for using their toll roads last time I drove through. That was with Michael, and I didn't know we were running prescription drugs across state lines. I'm not that type of person.

I met Robbie when I worked out of a wrinkled tent in a Hobby Lobby parking lot selling rugs and fake Persian carpets. You don't need skills to sell rugs. If someone asked for a price you'd just flip over the price tag and smile. That was my training. But I was the one who loaded them up inside the customer's vehicle. Smiling. Robbie pulled up in his worn-down Camry, riding on two spare tires - his entire ride drove with a limp, as if the frame had been folded, and when he drove over a dip in the concrete we all stopped and turned at the harsh sound of metal crunching up. He bought two rugs from us; I carried over two matching green rugs - a Fleur and a Rabia - and after we loaded it up in his car he asked if I was single.

I smiled because I was trained to do so and my manager once pulled a knife from her boot when I said, We have to smile to everyone? So I told Robbie yea. I was single. He asked if I liked working here and I said of course, even though I'd be quitting at the end of the week. Too fucking hot, and I hate working under the sun and smiling all day. Then, he told me in a smooth deep voice - his Bobby Caldwell impression, one of his many impressions after graduating from some ventriloquist program over the summer - he had a "thing" for me. And a whole lot to talk about, if I was interested.

I was. Or I wasn't, but I had nothing to do, nowhere else to go. I also thought Robbie was cute. A bit skinny, but I liked those rings he wore: a mix of gold and silver on every finger, with a sliver of blue or green shining in the middle. And he wore blue jeans like they were just another layer of skin. I didn't mind that. I asked him what he had in mind and he told me about music, about easy money. We moved the conversation to his car. He spoke of walking in, walking out, and being rich the very next day. He spoke of Rick James and I listened because it sounded better than selling rugs.

***

At around 2 p.m. the closing shift typically showed up. We were waiting to see who it would be today. A jeep pulled into the parking lot. It was Sad Sam's. I watched him stumble out of the vehicle while trying to carry what looked like a to-go coffee cup in one hand and a cellphone in the other. He used his knee to close the door - almost tripping backwards in the process, splashing coffee all over his hand and dropping the cup on the ground as he tried wiping his hands on his jeans. The commotion had the kid looking over, seeing what was going on. I nudged Robbie awake and told him it was Sad Sam's shift tonight.

"Cool. Actually, that's great. We can probably go through with everything tonight."

"Tonight?" I asked.

Robbie nodded. "Yep. I mean, so long as no one else clocks in. But that shouldn't happen. I'll make the call at 7:30 or so."

We sat together in silence as Robbie wasn't one to let gas waste, idling about without ever going anywhere. I rolled my window down about halfway. I listened to the sounds of the city. There were sirens, but there were always sirens; almost as constant as the quiet roar of tires treading past where we parked. I rested my head on the palm of my hand, elbow propped on the car door, and listened.

***

"Okay. I'm gonna call."

It was getting dark. The sky slowly morphed from a fiery orange to a dull, slow-blooming violet. I guess it was time. Robbie dug out his phone, but my focus remained outside. I checked the sidewalks. Empty. The kid was still there. I caught his outline through the occasional headlight, otherwise I'd lose him in the encroaching darkness. He sat with arms folded over his knees, watching the occasional car drive by. Grass covered his sneakers. Damn, we were really going to do this. Rick James, I told myself.

"Hello?" A voice crackled to life in the silence of the car. Robbie cleared his throat once, twice and began to talk in a deep voice that bounced around and vibrated my seat.

"Yes! Haha, hello!"

A pause ensued on the other end. Robbie and I traded glances.

"Is… Mr. Giacometti? Is that you, sir?"

Both of our shoulders slumped with relief. I didn't even realize how tight I was holding myself until I felt the tension unwind from my neck and shoulders. Part of me hoped it wouldn't work. I wanted Sad Sam to instantly catch on that this wasn't his boss. He'd realize it and hang up and this whole thing would be over. But I saw Robbie grinning, giving me a thumbs up.

"Yes! Haha, how are you, uh…?"

Oh, fuck. We didn't know his actual name. Robbie quickly reframed the question with, "HOW are you tonight, young man?"

"Um. Good, sir. How are you?"

Robbie gave a wave of his hand. "Oh fine, fine. Listen, I know it's a bit of a late notice, but I'll be dropping by to show a good friend of mine that 4001 Rickenbacker."

"Okay, sir. Would you like me to stick around after-hours?"

"That's nice of you, but once I get there you can leave. I'm not sure what time this fellow will show up. He's prone to appear before schedule, so if you can just keep him company until I arrive, well, that would be like a hot potato! Haha!"

I gave Robbie a look. He ignored it, shifting in his seat to look out the window. I still heard the voice on the end of the line speak.

"Sure thing, sir. What's your friend's name?"

"Mr. Collins. His name is Mr. Collins."

"Alright. I'll be on the lookout for him, sir."

Thank you, young man. Until then, take care. Stay classy, haha." Robbie hung up. He turned to me. I watched him release a great big sigh. "Holy shit."

I began unbuckling my seatbelt. "So who's making the grab? Me?"

"Yea. I'll follow in a little bit. Once I do, grab the guitar and run for it."

"We're meeting at the church over on Ivory Street."

"That's right. Stay on residential roads the entire way. Power walk, but don't run."

I opened the car door. "Okay." I tried getting out but a hand on my shoulder stopped me. I looked back to see Robbie bringing his hand around the back of my neck, pulling me towards him as he moved towards me. We met halfway in a brief kiss. His lips were warm and wet. I kept my eyes open so I knew Robbie had his closed. I watched him pull away and slowly open his eyes.

"Saw that in a mob movie. They did it before shit went down. Good luck."

I didn't reply. Just stepped out of the vehicle and gently closed the door. What movie had he been watching? The night was warm. Streetlights were on and drove away the shadows with spheres of orange I stepped through as I made my way down the street, stopping at the crosswalk before continuing, heading towards the music shop. It was so quiet. My steps were too loud. I looked behind me but no one was there. The street felt deserted, as if everyone agreed to call it for the night. It was me and my reflection from the windows I passed by. Up ahead, the kid remained sitting on the lawn.

I stopped. The door to the music store was only a couple paces away, on my right. Had he seen me? He didn't look my way, not yet, but I didn't know if that would be the case as I'm making a getaway, white guitar in hand and who knows what else happening. He could tell the police. I didn't bring a mask. Why the fuck did this plan not include masks? I should tell him to leave. I could go over and say, Hello, you don't know me but it's dark (as you can tell, hopefully) and you should hurry on home because tonight is a school night and you will need your sleep. He'd look at me with starry-eyed wonder - he forgot! - and quickly get up and run all the way back home, yelling thank you thank you thank you.

Pushing the door open, I stepped inside. A bell rang somewhere above. Music played from speakers I couldn't see. The smell of incense washed over me. I looked to the side and saw a stick burning slowly in a brass holder from atop a glass case filled with shiny effects pedals. There were miniature stands with packets of guitar picks and strings lined up, on display. Someone stood behind the counter with their back turned to me. They were in the process of hanging a cherry red guitar on the wall. Upon hearing the bell, however, they quickly finished the job and turned to greet me. I found myself looking at Sad Sam up close for the first time. He wore glasses too. I called him Sad Sam because when I first watched him he was receiving a ticket for illegally parking on the street (the parking lot was full) while the city cleaned the roads. He looked normal, I could see that now. Skinny. Kind of cute.

"Hi there," he said to me.

"Hey."

"Are you Mr. Collins?"

I stared at him. "Yea. Yes. I'm a friend of your boss, Giacometti." I waved at him. "Hi." Sad Sam nodded at me as he moved things around the display.

"Nice to meet you. Mr. Giacometti said you'd be visiting. The Rickenbacker is just right there." He raised a hand and pointed somewhere behind me. I followed the gesture to a small round table set up close to the center of the store, from which a guitar stand was placed. Resting in the plastic grip of the stand was the 4001 Rickenbacker.

"Feel free to have a look."

I didn't reply. Instead, I walked over for a closer look. The store's carpeting - a soft lavender color - masked the sound of my steps. Posters were nailed on every available surface, the faces of guitarists, singers, and famous songwriters watching me. But I was staring at the guitar. It wasn't exactly white, but a creamy off-white. Like egg shells. Pure white made me think of a doctor's office, of sterile lighting. This thing had life, even if no one was currently playing it. I couldn't play any instrument, but damn if I didn't want to pick it up and try. I reached for its neck.

Damn. Rick James.

The bell above the door gave another ring. I heard Sad Sam address the newcomer with the same level of enthusiasm he showed me.

"Hi there."

"Hello." It was Robbie. My heart quickened.

"How can I help you?"

"By staying right fucking there."

I wrapped my hand around the guitar's neck and lifted it off the stand. It was surprisingly heavy. Or maybe it wasn't. I didn't know. But it did come free with no restriction. Now in my grip, I used my other hand to hold on near its bottom. Without looking at either one of them, I calmly walked toward the door as Robbie continued staring down Sad Sam, who remained still and silent behind the counter. Robbie moved to the side to let me bump open the door with my shoulder. I remained careful not to damage the guitar. Rick James, damn.

Somewhere between my first step out the door and my last step inside the shop itself, the large window overlooking the street exploded. Glass shattered, followed by a series of metal clangs like a pipe rolling down the street. I looked over, spotted a bat glinting under the street light as it rolled across the road and was stopped by the rise of pavement indicating the sidewalk.

I twisted around to find Robbie looking at Sad Sam, so I followed suit. Sad Sam stared back at us, his hands trembling and a look of fright twisting his normal face.

"I'm sorry," he told us, crouching down as if grabbing something, returning to view just a second later with another metal baseball bat. He raised it above his head.

Robbie shoved his way through, nearly tearing the door off its hinges as he raced outside. I caught a glimpse of his face and saw only terror. I don't think he even looked at me as he started running down the street, back towards the car. I ran before I knew I was running. Maybe I screamed, or perhaps my through grew sore from trying to swallow down the fear. I was running down the street but I couldn't see the car. It wasn't there! I didn't see Robbie, either. I noticed the little kid look up at my sudden appearance and I immediately understood, through flashing images seared across my brain. I ran the wrong way.

Was there a right way for someone like me? After something like this, everything - every step - felt wrong. Instead of dwelling on the thought I pushed it to the side and settled in to observe myself scooping the kid up by the waist - all while continuing forward. I switched my grip on the guitar to rest solely in my left hand, allowing me a better handle with the person I now carried to my right like a sack of flour.

He didn't say a word. Neither did I. We just ran down the street together, him hobbling along silently. I wished he would've said something. Maybe, Why did you kidnap me? And I would explain to him, Little kids such as yourself shouldn't be exposed to violence, and this is actually called saving your life. Maybe he'd thank me. Or quit squirming so I could run faster.

To be honest I wasn't sure if Sad Sam was even following us. Perhaps he felt his mission accomplished at scaring us away from stealing more items. I could hear only the pounding of blood in my ears. It pulsed with every step. Soon we reached the end of the bloc and I cut right, down a different street. It was residential, and most of the houses had their porch light turned on. Silhouette glided across the windows. I didn't think about stopping until we made it past several houses. Then my senses caught up with me and I felt winded. I gently set the kid down and stepped back, trying to regain my breath.

My fingers were wrapped painfully around the guitar's neck. The boy watched me with silent, wide eyes. I looked back at him, my breathing barely more than grunts. We stared at one another. I motioned to him with the guitar.

"Stay in school," was all I said. I moved to walk past him, ready to become lost in a suburban maze so I could think about what to do next - what is *next* for someone in my position - when I heard a shrill voice break the silence of the night.

"Wha- Just what in the absolute hell!"

I turned around. So did the boy. We watched a figure appear in the doorway to the house we stood in front of. Light spilled forth as it was opened further, then slammed shut, followed by the shuffling of feet. Slippers, I thought to myself. It was a woman - an older woman - wearing slippers and dressed in a nightgown - that looked as stuffy as a rug I would've sold - quickly approaching us.

"Cliff!" she called out. "Is that you, boy?!"

The little boy beside me started walking towards her. But she had eyes for me only. I noticed her digging around in a large purse cradled in the crook of one of her arms. I looked from the purse back to her. There was a snarl etched into her weathered face, adding an extra layer of wrinkles to her forehead and around her mouth.

"You goddamn freak! Trying to kidnap my baby, are you?!"

I wanted to tell her, No, in fact I just rescued the child that you let wander around with supervision. Are you his mother? Mother's don't let their kids be alone where they can be exposed to bats being thrown through windows or theft. She pulled something out of her purse before I had a chance to say any of that and jammed the object into my stomach - moving surprisingly fast. After a soft *click* I felt my insides violently convulse as if someone grabbed them, twisted them together, all while digging in with their teeth. I was being electrocuted. This old woman was shocking the fuck out of me. Despite this revelation, I still wondered, Where was the boy? I imagined him watching - or perhaps he had already chosen a spot in the yard and sat down - as I spasmed out. Another crime for him to witness. The old woman was so close I could smell coffee on her breath. Or maybe human flesh smells like coffee when being tazed. Regardless, I wanted to grab her and tell her to, Quit, goddamnit! Your child is watching! Do you want them to grow up normal? Or become one of those idiots who runs around with the first person to throw attention their way?

No, it was too late for this woman. She continued holding down the trigger. I couldn't see as my eyes rolled into the back of my head, but I could still feel the effects of her labor. I truly felt sorry for that kid if he was here. Clearly this woman - a mom, a grandma, a failure - didn't give a damn about him. If I could, I'd tell the boy myself. I'd tell him, Go pick up an instrument and learn it. Do you like music? You do now. Do you know Rick James? He played guitar. Bass, actually. Do you want to learn bass? You do now. And then he wouldn't wander around. He'd know where to go. Or, more importantly, he would understand where not to go, because that is just as important.

Lillo Way

of love

my son will take his warmest outerwear
or he won't I won't
remind him
it is cold in Wisconsin.

last year's datebook wildflowers
by name. this year it's mushrooms
so crazy-looking I think
I am one of them.

I hear a poet ask what one would choose
blessed or lucky. the next poet opts
for whichever will turn her into the blue
of the sky.

for one week my son
lets me into his tiny apartment
his animal's den. he who
is an addict. he who was born
from my body. under unlucky stars.

now the wall's gone up.
no choice but to wait. a gap
between the stones between
the granite clouds.
if I'm lucky.

days push their way
into weeks in which I cannot
write nor read nor speak
to any soul. shrieking
winds. relentless rain. I resume

the dig. two volcanic mountains
of clothes, one he calls clean,
one dirty. his childhood quilt
next to an altar piled with a hundred
lucky things and fifty dollar bills
he might have used to pay the bills.

I gather the ends
of cigarettes, notes, coins,
syringe, bent spoon, spheres
of dirt, strata of grease.

hands and knees tough up. heart
and mind splinter into one another.
I'm a backache laborer
of love.

Laura Alderson

War Time

Majuro Atoll, 1944

You are chatting on the beach, relaxed
because there is a ferocious war going on at sea
but today the men are camped peacefully in the sand on this Pacific
      island
and you, an ensign, have brought candy from the ship
for native children who have never had it.
They swarm you.
The chief of the island people comes
and you start a casual conversation
because what else do you do
after the captain of your heavy cruiser
a day ago had said
Men, when we land
there will be hand-to-hand combat.
You had taken out the .45 the Navy issued
weighed its heft and wondered
if your hand would shake.

When you land on this island
the enemy have left
and God the relief in that.
Not at sea, no longer listening to
thunder beyond a horizon orange and pink with explosions.
At sea, your captain called the men together
the night before battle to say
Gentlemen, we expect to be in combat tomorrow and
we believe your chances of survival are around forty percent
and you considered how badly you would be burned
because fire is what kills you on a heavy cruiser in the Pacific
that is a huge floating target for suicide bombers.
So you talk with this tribal chief of the Marshall Islands.
It is hot. You hear his accent and he explains

he was sent to Oxford University in England
in preparation for leading his people who took up a collection to
send him.
And you offhandedly ask as the sand warms your feet
what he liked most about England. He falls silent
which seems to be his way. Then he replies in pleasant English
The calendar.
That you can know where you are in the days.

N. G. Haiduck

A Cat Named Sonny Truitt

"Tell them to bring their horns," Sonny had said to his oldest daughter April as he was dying of cancer. And so she had invited all of his musician friends to come to his house in Queens for a memorial party on a Saturday afternoon in November 1995.

"Have lots of food and lots of drink," he had instructed, and so his son Clement, a professional chef, had prepared a spread.

Sonny was my husband Neal's supervisor at ASCAP, the American Society of Composers, Authors and Publishers. On Neal's first day at ASCAP – his first office gig, not counting playing for corporate parties and a stint as a night watchman – Sonny took him aside and said: "You are going to learn this job. You know why? Because this is a good job." Neal took Sonny's words to heart. That steady gig at ASCAP paid off the mortgage on our Bronx bungalow and sent our daughter to Catholic school.

Sonny was greatly admired at ASCAP for his knowledge and experience in jazz, and because he was a gentleman. He learned saxophone and piano as a youth, but picked up the trombone when he found one on the deck of a Navy destroyer during World War II. After the War, Sonny, whose given name was Sumner, went to Boston to study at Schillinger House, the forerunner of the Berklee School of Music. He made the Boston jazz scene, rooming with pianist Bill Fontaine and playing trombone, tenor sax, and piano with be-boppers Serge Chaloff, Charlie Mariano, Richard Twardzick, Nat Pierce.

He left Boston in 1953 and came to New York, where he played with Charlie Parker, Oscar Pettiford, Chubby Jackson, Phil Woods, Claude Thornhill, Buddy Rich. He recorded on trombone with Miles Davis, who remembered "a cat named Sonny Truitt" in his autobiography.

He was not a virtuoso player; he didn't throw a lot of notes at you, but he was a beautiful player, original, melodic, and modern.

He was a talented arranger, writing for Neal Hefti, Tony Scott, Bill Evans. He took the job at ASCAP in 1963. He had three children: April, Clement, and Sarah. He and his wife were divorced.

Neal and Sonny became friends when Sonny asked Neal for a few lessons on the classical clarinet. Neal was honored. Every lunch hour, they found an empty room at ASCAP and practiced clarinet duets. It was a peaceful respite from the work day. Even as Sonny became sick, the noontime clarinet sessions continued.

I first met him when we all went to hear Buddy DeFranco and Terry Gibbs at Fat Tuesdays. I saw him last when we paused at the Lincoln Center plaza one July evening, a few months before he died, to catch Bob Wilber's big band, playing swing music from the '40s. Bob spotted Sonny before the set started. "Hey, Man, how are you doing?"

"Not too good. I've been spending all my time trying to get well."

Sonny was wearing crisp khaki Bermuda shorts, knee socks, a golf shirt, and Rockport walking shoes. He was clutching *The Wall Street Journal*, coming from work at ASCAP across Broadway. He was 72 years old, had a round, open face, usually rosy, but now pale and puffy, usually creased with a wide grin, but now a frown. Bob nodded soberly, shook his hand, "Good luck, Man," and climbed back on the bandstand.

Sonny ducked into the subway on Broadway and headed home to Queens. We listened to the first set and watched the swing dancers in their swing costumes, full skirts, bobby socks and saddle shoes. It might have been fun, except that we felt so sad.

And now Neal and I were standing in front of the Tudor-style gray stone row house that Sonny had inherited from his second wife, who had died some years ago. April opened the door and greeted us with Sonny's wide grin. She had name tags for everyone, which I thought was a good idea.

Sonny's favorite aunt was there. Sonny's brother was there. His grandchildren, Clement's children, were there. The food was set up buffet style in the dining room. Clement and his tall blond wife were busy bringing out the dishes: pasta with a pink tomato and cream sauce, sausage and peppers, a mesculun salad, breads, cakes. There was plenty of sangria and beer. People were smiling, shaking hands, introducing themselves.

A drum set and bass were crammed beside an electric keyboard at the far end of the living room. Gray-haired men were sitting on folding chairs, opening up instrument cases, pulling out saxophones and trumpets. Neal shook hands with Dick Meldonian, a skinny guy with a gray ponytail and a walrus mustache, a Stan Kenton alumnus who had a gleaming Selmer tenor sax hanging around his neck. It was Sonny's horn. Neal took a seat, opened up his case, put his clarinet together.

Bill Fontain, a handsome man with white hair, sat down at the keyboard. Another slim, white-haired gentleman got comfortable behind the bass. Drummer Ed Bonoff picked up his sticks and straddled his long legs around the drums. An old timer named Carl, an ugly fellow with a big smile, put his trumpet to his mouth. Mickey Golumb, a jovial little man wearing his boating shoes, joined in on tenor sax. The music began and didn't stop.

"Swinging grandpas," Neal called them. One would take a break, "running out to smoke pot," said Neal, and another would take his place, playing jazz standards, taking solos. Neal, 50, was the youngest.

Meldonian played Sonny's tenor sax until well after the sun had set. Neal explained to me later: "He even used Sonny's mouthpiece. You never use another musician's mouthpiece. Borrow my horn, but leave me my mouthpiece. He even used Sonny's reed."

I wondered how his children felt to see all these friends of their father's whom they didn't know, yet we all knew them, from various conversations with Sonny. April, Clement, and Sarah were sitting together on the staircase, listening raptly to the music.

I crossed the room, squeezing between people sitting or standing, tapping their feet to the beat, and shouting approval. "Yeah, Dick!" "Go, Mickey!"

"Your father would have loved the party," I said when I reached the staircase.

"We never heard him play music," said April. "Did we?" she asked Clement.

"No," said Clement. "He didn't share that with us."

"But I wish he had," said Sarah. "I wish we could have enjoyed this before."

"He was a piece of jazz history," I said.

April nodded, smiling, "We know."

The tune, "How High the Moon," ended and everybody clapped and cheered.

Greg Nelson

On the Pier Above the Nansemond River

Leaning on the weathered railing,
standing in the warm sun or the brisk wind,
watching the current roil or glide
and the sky do as it pleases,

though far from overjoyed with the world and myself,
I'm at peace with all I see. Months pass
between boats. The best moment came
one summer evening, when dozens lined the pier.

The sun was setting over the island of trees,
and the great egret sailing along the shore,
a god made of snow, turned to gold.
We raised our phones like an offering

to the ageless spirit descending
over us. The river remains sacred
to the Nansemond Indian Nation.
If imperfectly, we understood why.

Mark Smith-Soto

First *Teléfono*

Cero, siete, nueve, no area code then,
just the three digits easy for a boy
to memorize for an emergency,

a number that tethers
to a long, narrow pink adobe house
where one day the hunched, horned,

black box appeared perched
on a little table, alert, poised to deliver
shock after shock to the air, black

plastic, hard and heavy in the hand,
heavy in a new way, serious
with alarm and accident,

it roosted tilting a bit as if to fly
off the handle once and for all
with electric news, the dog run over,

an aunt abandoned, the living room
where we played hide and seek
thrown open to a world on the brink.

Kevin Winchester

The Bones in Ravenna

"Can I draw on your board?" he asks, "Ms. Anderson and Ms. Martin have stuff they need to keep on theirs."

I don't know him, don't recall seeing him in the hallways. He looks sixteen, maybe seventeen; a junior or senior. School issue mask. He's tall, not thin but not muscular, either; his skin the polished caramel of a buckeye, his hair a mop of short braids above a high and tight like all the kids are wearing. Nothing to separate him from the crowd, nothing I'd remember.

The room is empty and I glance at the whiteboard. My words, "SYMBOLS: WHITE, GOLD, SUNSET, MIDNIGHT," underlined. My students' suggestions, "purity, good, weight, richness, death, endings, sinister, new beginnings," scrawled in loose columns below. Random marks, terms, directional arrows, phrases: Poe and gothic, individualism and hope, Make It New—my notes and the kids' comments on American Romanticism weave around the columns. Wednesday. Been a long day, a long week, and yet… Wednesday. I'd planned to copy, or at least leave the student responses in order to revisit them tomorrow when we start on the Poe pieces.

But…kids. They all want something these days. Expect it. But somehow, I don't know, by now I assumed there'd be… *more.* More success, more answers, more clarity. More time. Twenty years teaching at the University left me unsated and disillusioned but still mildly entertained. Then, this pandemic erased the rules, moved the proverbial goalposts. In the midst of it, I published my research, not that anyone noticed, and soon after that, my mother passed. Nothing felt real anymore. So, when this teaching opportunity at the high school came up, I figured, why not? Make a difference, touch a life. Right. Dire Straits warned us—money for nothing, get your kicks for free—and here I am. Christ, I'm getting old.

I look at him, waiting, his dark eyes prayerful. "Sure," I tell him, thinking I'll remember the examples my kiddos suggested but knowing I won't. I toss him the cloth I've been using to clean the whiteboards and go back to my notes.

I sense him wiping the board, peripherally, and instantly ignore him, focus instead on highlighting sections of the Coleridge essay I'll bore them with tomorrow. A moment later, I'm startled as he appears in front of me again. "Yes?" I ask.

"Do you have any markers?"

Damn, kid. In one way, his audacity impresses me. In another, it pisses me off. Maybe it's a lingering Covid side-effect. They've been out of the classroom for almost two years. They might be juniors, but they have the academic maturity of freshmen, at best. All of them. Screw it, I'm tired.

"Certainly. What color do you prefer?"

He shifts his weight, juts his hip to the left, and the sarcasm flies right by him.

"Black and blue. If you have them."

I crack open my drawer, hoping to retrieve a couple markers without him seeing the unopened eighteen-pack… but I fail.

"Oh," he says, "can I have a purple and pink, too? And that orange? If there's a red in there—" He stops, shifts his weight, and his hip, back to center, deferring. "I'm sorry. Whatever you have is fine," he says.

I first went to Italy back in the nineties. Did the whole tourist tour—Venice, Florence, Rome. Saw the Sistine Chapel just after the ceiling and Last Judgement restoration. Mostly luck, partly planning, I was there mid-week, in the morning, and the crowds were relatively small. I stood in the center of the great hallway, craning my neck and head backward, and the sheer power of it, the magnitude of detail and color made me numb. Not desensitized, but physically numb. I couldn't feel my body; lost all sense of anyone else being in the room. I needed another word beyond sublime. Something more visceral. Something that ached more. Something that described how completely the work absorbed me and I it. I'm no artist, can't draw water from a well, but somehow I knew, I felt the painstaking experience of creating, of imagining. Why not, I think, let's see how the magic happens, and I hand him the entire pack of markers.

"Knock yourself out," I tell him.

He bounces away and I return to the essay and the next day's lesson plans. The plans are a challenge, something I'm not used to doing. College was different; I'd been at it so long. Lecture prep occurred walking across the quad to class. I knew the material. Students got it or they didn't. In the real world, people fail. Not in High School, not anymore. Nothing lower than a fifty. Multiple re-takes. It's not really due until grades are posted. I don't know how to package the material for that, don't know how to sell it. *Break it up, small sections, no more than twenty minutes of anything*, the admin tells me. *Keep them entertained*. They're coddled, helpless, and lacking of curiosity. And we're making it worse every day.

I'm completely retooling everything—worksheets, projects, content, all of it. Lectures don't work. I realized quickly, these aren't just younger students, they're Covid kids. Covid kids raised by helicopter parents and high-graphic video games. The willing suspension of disbelief needs a new definition and I struggle, daily, to find it. They didn't want Coleridge, they wanted Kid Cudi. The philosophical realism of Virginia Woolf? Nope, Taylor Swift's ten minute version of "All Too Well" dropped today. Symbol, simile, and tone? Addison Rae just posted a new TikTok. Assignments? Fortnite missions. I lean back in my chair, clench my eyes closed.

When I open them, the kid is standing a few feet away from the board, hands on his hips, a brown marker—my marker—dangling from his lips like an off-brand Robusto. He's filled nearly half my whiteboard. It's a bust, a portrait of some kind, I think. His body blocks most of it and he's drawn horizontal and vertical lines in a grid over the entire thing. Maybe a jail, prison bars, who knows? He's also drawn several random circles in certain sections, a couple near what I think are the eyes, and another near the cheek, another near the crown of the head.

I don't get it. It's flat, one dimensional, and void of emotion, but somehow, I get the sense he's pleased with his effort. The gridlines and circles give the whole thing a sterile look, institutional even. I don't know, maybe he's going for some futuristic theme, something video game inspired. Whatever it is, it reminds me how deep the chasm lies between me and these kids. Every day I look for some point of connection, some common ground, a way in. Been a long time since I was in high school. At sixteen, we started watching draft numbers. The casualty counts on the nightly news provided the backdrop for all we did. Sure, dating, sports, cars, music, they filled our world too, but we…we… we seemed so much *older* then. These kids…everything seems superficial, their lives vapid routines…and it doesn't bother them in the least. I don't get it.

And now I'm frustrated with lesson planning. Pearls before swine. The student puts the marker on the desk, picks up the cloth, and starts humming as he steps back to the board. I think he's going to erase the whole thing, start over, or just abandon it altogether, but he doesn't. Instead, he begins to rub away the gridlines. He moves quickly at first, broad swipes, but each done with focused intent. He slows as he nears the features of the bust, the face, then resumes. I lean to one side and I realize what he's done. I had the order wrong. I assumed he'd done the lines after he'd drawn the face, but he hadn't. He drew them first; the grid helped him with proportions, with symmetry.

He wipes away the circles with the rag and I know they were drawn ahead of time as well. The picture takes on more dimension as he erases. Still a bit flat and I don't see much emotion in the expression, but it at least looks like somebody, like a normal person. He drops the rag. It misses the desktop completely, falls to the floor, but he doesn't notice. He leans into the board, his face nearly touching the one he's drawn, and begins to smudge away small sections with his fingertips. A segment here, gone; an arc to the right and above it disappears.

As he works, I realize I'm leaning forward too, my breath shallow and tight. I'm anxious, as if I now have something invested in the work, in its completion. I still don't see emotion in the drawing, it's only dry erase on a whiteboard, but the emotion in the room is palpable. The erasing, the taking away makes everything more clear, brings everything into sharper focus. He takes several steps back. "There," he says. It's as if the word is not spoken, but rather, it escapes.

The drawing is simple yet clear. A face. Female. The head turned slightly toward me, chin nestled on her hand, her fingers lightly touch her cheek. The hand is exquisite, the best part of the drawing by far. The detail in the knuckles, the proportions. Kid's done this before. The string of a mask drapes between her index and middle finger, the mask itself falls past her wrist. It's purple with pink designs throughout. Beside her hand, the lips. Full, partially opened as if she's just spoken, or is about to say something important. The corners of her mouth turned up, more than a Mona Lisa smile, but not a happy smile, either. The nose is slightly off, but her eyes are direct. Not a lot of detail, not a lot of depth, but I'm drawn to them. I'm not sure if I've ever used this word before, not in its truest sense, but the eyes look weary.

The whole thing makes me suddenly uncomfortable. I'm in the middle of something personal, and I don't know what to say, or if I should say anything at all. The kid is nonplussed. He saunters to my desk, one hand digging in his coat pocket.

"I have two Jolly Ranchers," he says, "do you like cherry or watermelon?"

"I'm not… I don't…"

"Here. Please. Take them both."

He stretches his hand toward me, palm up. I look at the candy, look back up at him, then take the cherry one. "Thank you," I say.

"Thank *you*," he smiles. "I needed to draw."

I nod. "It's nice, it's nice," I offer, still uneasy. "I mean, she's nice, the drawing."

"My Moms," he smiles bigger. "She got Covid last year. Sometimes, I think I've forgotten the sound of her voice and I get panicky. Drawing makes it better, I can hear her again."

Michelangelo's tomb is at the Basilica of Santa Croce in Florence. So are Machiavelli, Galileo, Rossini, and Dante's. I paused at each, trying to absorb the magnitude of the contributions, take the measure of what paradigmatic forces they were, the sway they still held. Solitary, mortal men. I tried to imagine them as ordinary guys, guys who worked and laughed and loved and over-ate and worried about the weather. But did they doubt? Did they question themselves? Their choices? In the middle of it all, did they realize their impact? Their worth? I wish I knew.

Of course, I lingered at Dante's vault. The bowed *Poetry* in mourning on his right, the finely sculpted *Italy* standing to his left, pointing upward to the marbled Poet himself, seated in contemplation atop the structure—beautiful, stunning even, but it paled in comparison to his writing. The exquisite symmetry, the perfection in Cantos and numerology, the precision of meter and rhyme. The pointed wit, the score-settling, the reverence and dedication, the lyrical beauty, the imagination, the lasting effect. One poem solidified an entire national language, for God's sake. The Florentine leaders awarded the job to Rizzo but Dante's work so impressed Michelangelo, the painter wanted to design and sculpt his sarcophagus. I wanted to believe it was true; after all, wasn't the Sistine Chapel Michelangelo's attempt to portray in paint the same wonder and terror and hope Dante portrayed on the page?

But Dante didn't know of his impact, he had no designs to be remembered for centuries to come. Couldn't have. He did it all as a tribute for his dear Beatrice, for his beloved Florence, and nothing more. And yet, his love for Beatrice remained unrequited, his exile from Florence still intact, for his bones lie somewhere in Ravenna. His Florence sarcophagus waits empty, filled only with his grief.

The young man stands silent before me, waiting to be excused. I nod and mumble that he can come back anytime, anytime he needs to. He thanks me again and leaves. I stare at the image on the board and weep, his footsteps echoing down the empty hallway.

David E. Poston

No Cello, No Lamb, No Rosemary

No cello, no lamb, no rosemary—
a cool cellar and a sycamore tree.

The sycamore tree he climbs with cousins
while aunts and uncles watch from the porch.

He watches Masons drop roses on his uncle's casket.
Is this how a born-again life closes? A circle

from cool cellar to sycamore tree to casket?
Zacchaeus, come down from there!

His life turns to *Amazing Grace* sung in
a white-washed chapel in the piney woods.

Zacchaeus comes down, and then there
is nowhere to hide as the hymn rings out

in the white-washed chapel in the pines.
No cello, no lamb, no rosemary—snowflakes

on gray marble, his mother pulling sandspurs
from his bare feet, salmon cakes on Saturdays.

His grandmother's wringer washer smells of soap,
the clay of her dugout cellar cool under his toes.

On the long school-bus ride from town,
the voices of his mother and his four uncles

fade as he imagines the tower of Babel falling,
his cousins tumbling from the sycamore tree.

Around him the others jostle and snicker.
He watches his small white face glide past the pines.

Vivian I. Bikulege

Pottery

I throw pots
slam clay onto a wheel
center hope
form vessels
trim imagination.

Norma Bourland

Stitching Time

The sun feels soothing on my winter-dried face as it tries to permeate the room through the window panes in my 7th-floor living room. I welcome it with a whisper beneath my breath as I settle into my favorite blue wingback chair. With a familiar rhythm, I push my needle in and out of the cloth that drapes across my lap, down my knees and onto the floor. I welcome the distraction from this pensive task that allows time for loose thoughts to join together much like these running stitches themselves.

I heard the news last night. My second son, now a grown man, faces a new beginning all alone. I am far away from him. I do what I know to do, what I can do, what I think will say I believe in you. It's my prayer pieced together in black and white strips like the dark colorless days of his wayward journey. The strips of varied patterns will come together as a cover over the past with a bright red, soft flannel underside to say: begin again. With the strength of the running stitch, the old and the new are held together as I sew in time-tested wisdom, memories, and worn-out prayers with each stitch. I will give it to him as a gift, then stand back and await the magic only a quilt creates.

The soft cloth submits to my fingers, and the stitches begin to line up, creating a road of sorts, going in the direction I determine. The harmony between my mind and hands allows the past to surface like a jack-in-a-box when the lid opens.

"Remember that small bedroom with windows on one wall, the one I shared with my sister?" I ask myself as if I'm chatting with a friend. I can feel that small sun-filled room of long ago when I'd sit on the floor and lay my doll on the fabric scrap I'd taken from Mother's sewing basket. With big sewing scissors in my small hands

I would cut around the form to get the pieces for a dress or kimono or whatever I fancied. Does anyone have a sewing basket today, I wonder? Do children still learn how to sew by making clothes for their dolls? I've heard that knitting has come into vogue with kids nowadays. But I like the feel of fabric. All kinds. Slippery satin, coarse raw muslin, warm fuzzy wool, crisp cotton, and this cozy flannel underneath the cotton pieces that will finish this quilt. Much better than knitting yarn.

I think of my two little boys on *their* bedroom floor, not sewing for dolls, but playing with blocks and Legos, making cities and forts and whatever they imagined. Two brothers, a year apart in age, both from my body, so close yet so different. They shared so much time together. When they went in their own directions, one went with smooth even strides and purposeful steps, the other with uneven strides in chaotic directions and missteps along the way.

Today, though, in *this* sun-filled room, my needle continues in the direction of hope for another new beginning.

I know the path of my own running stitch, from doll clothes to school clothes, from prom dress to wedding veil, from baby blankets and mother-daughter dresses, from hemmed-up track pants and Halloween costumes, quilts and curtains. I know that old faithful running stitch is like the stitch of time, where the rhythm of day in and day out often plays old beats to new lyrics and makes roads less straight in unfamiliar directions, directions I *don't* determine.

When time, like my needle, moves steadily at the hands of a more gifted designer than I and uses new patches to cover the frays of my unintentional rips, there's wholeness. A broken relationship, a scary health change, a rebellious child, a devastating relocation, a drastic change in vocation all rip the fabric and require patient mending, require stitching in a new direction.

Norma Bourland **109**

Starting fresh with bright new fabric is always easier than taking the old and redirecting the seams to make them fit a new shape. But what a wonder when the old *is* reborn by careful patching or by weaving it into the new as if it had never been torn away, and the past is not lost. It is work to make the pieces fit back together. I wonder if he knows this. I wonder if he knows that each stitch matters. Not by itself. It matters only when each one adds to the other to join the pieces into something whole.

In and out. Not in a hurry. No use counting. The number doesn't matter. It's the process, the journey. Each stitch helps create the journey. Sometimes a knot interrupts the running stitch. Sometimes a back stitch is necessary to strengthen the gaps. Sometimes just a different color of thread.

And like each stitch, each year matters. I count them by the age of the silver thimble I saw my Granny use, and the old pair of scissors on the table next to the red tomato pin cushion that belonged to my mother. My hands, not as nimble as once they were, cramp easily. They demand I stretch my fingers every few moments. I notice the thin skin and exposed veins on my hands, like those on the hands that once taught me many years ago.

He counts his years by time-served, by good behavior or rehab programs completed, and mostly by time lost from family, friends and freedom.

The rhythm of my running stitch continues, the sun and time do too. In and out. My threaded needle sews the stitches of the past with today while the warm sunny morning fills the room. My spirit cheers as it sheds light and warmth into the dreary corners of the past night and exposes my lifetime of stitching, my stitching a lifetime, *our* lifetime.

Joyce Schmid

Floodlit

As a child, my sister made up plays,
herself director, editor, and star,
princess of a cast of china statuettes.
Her inch-wide headboard was our stage.
We'd kneel with her behind her bed
and reach to slide the figures back and forth
across their narrow wooden world
for our imagined audience.
Summon the princess to my royal bed.
We'd speak her lines, but there were no asides.
"Out of the game…" we'd beg, and she,
in princess voice, would answer us: "*What game?*"

She was to write *I cringe to bare my being in a public place…*
I will] pretend I am alone…more private
in imagined privacy. For her, it was a choice
to live or not live in reality.

She married her first husband young,
beside him when he got his PhD at twenty-three in Math.
She wrote to him, *You've made your life and mine so real to me,*
That I'm made subject to reality,
but then took off her glasses, left him,
and went off to Hollywood.
She opted not to see. She just unveiled her eyes—
blue, beautiful, with flecks of gold.

Today--a shock—my baby sister old,
leached hair and ruined skin,
those storied eyes confused.
She clashes with her image
like an oboe out of tune.
Maestro, true the note.

Turn down the light, give her
her trademark hat, the one
that swirls around her face,
and she will be the way she used to be
when Nobel winners looked at her and sighed,
and Hollywood and Vine came out in stars
to watch her going by.

And now she's dying in her brain
where she had always longed to live.
She says *"They're feeding me unholy water"*
but *" Some people here are nice."*
She says, *"Goodbye- I'm needed on the set."*
She can't remember what she's doing
even while she's doing it—
my little sister, flickering,
gold blanched to white in her blue eyes,
an inmate of her dreams at last.

Note: Italicized lines are from poems by Dolly Garter
Gordon, used with permission.

Mary Ann Crowe

Inheritance

Sticks and stones my mother would say and likely pray that
names would never hurt us—*see, no broken bones*—when
we lived a mile from Carson McCullers's home near the big

muddy red clay Chattahoochie and a redhead named Rusty
called me *Red* and because I was the only one in our family
of four he claimed I was *adopted, your father isn't really*

your father which led my real mother to show me her old
art book with finely printed hand-glued plates of Flemish
paintings of Madonnas with hair the color of her Belgian

aunts and angels and Botticelli's Venus the color of mine
an art historical lesson for a five-year-old on recessive
genes in a family of none I could see with hair like me

Evelyn Menary

Lucky Strike

There had not been such a lot of commotion on Lucky Strike Farm on a single day in maybe a century – or, for that matter, in forever. There were pickup trucks, huge stock trucks and cars parked off the long lane and scattered throughout the fields. Some women had laid out a picnic on the lowered tailgates of their trucks. Kids ran in all directions, shouting and tripping over yapping dogs.

Outside of the imposing barn, a cowboy-hatted, tight-jeaned man stood atop an empty wagon rack. He clasped his hand kind of gentle-like around a microphone close to his mouth. He was rattling off a speedy language that a growing crowd attended to, as if at a revival meeting.

Everybody knew everybody pretty well, the only exception being a tall, thin, middle-aged man in a white cambric shirt which he'd unbuttoned due to the heat of the day. He sported a pair of brand-new looking dark green farmer pants. No hat; that alone made him stand out among the bobbing motion of farmer caps and cowboy hats. The outsider and now owner of the land, Doctor Price, was oblivious to those around him muttering to one another and tilting their heads in his direction.

"Is that the brother?" some of them said.

"Is that the Doc?" others asked.

"Haven't seen him around here since he was a young'un," one said.

"Ay-dibba-dibba,
igotsevenfiveseventyfivewhosegonnagivemeonehundred,

ay-dibba-dibbgoingoncegoingtwice," the auctioneer called.

Doctor Price studied the crowd and the auctioneer, trying to discern who was bidding; but, for the life of him, he couldn't figure it out. He raised his hand to wipe the sweat from his brow.

"Sold to Dr. Price!" shouted the auctioneer. The crowd broke into collective mirth and everyone stared at Price.

"Just joshing ya' Doc!" said the salesman. "Sold to MacDonough for one hundred dollars!"

People were restless because every tiddly thing from the house was being auctioned off first. Most of them were here to buy the livestock – the fat Hereford cattle milling nervously in corrals, pigs in pens that were rooting up the ground and even the loose chickens pecking at the dirt all around the farm yard.

Even so, something made the bidders perk up with interest. A banged up brown pickup was raising dust as it drove way too fast into the long lane; it lurched to a stop right between the farm machinery and the auction wagon.

"Dan," the crowd murmured to itself.

Dan had a bulky build which powered him through the crowd. His curly brown hair, sprouting from the sides of his gas station cap, matched his scruffy beard. A cigarette hung out of his mouth and he was breathing hard, both nostrils blowing out smoke like those of a cartoon bull.

The story made its way around the crowd as the auctioneer began to sell some dishware.

"I heard tell that Dan got left the acreage down the road, but the Doc got the home farm. All because their father was so mad at Dan before the end," said a man in denim overalls.

"Well – Dan *did* damn near burn the barn down – worst you can *do* on a farm," asserted a man in red plaid.

"Who'd a thought, though, that the son who stayed on and helped out would get some scrubby land with no buildings, while the one who took off first chance got the farm?" a green-plaid-wearing farmer pondered.

"Kind of a prodigal son thing," a fellow in brown plaid added thoughtfully. The others looked at him and at each other, not knowing what to say.

Dan steamed right up to the face of his taller brother and began cussing. It was then that the auctioneer grabbed back the attention of the crowd.

"Listen up!" he said, "You're not going to want to miss this! Next on auction will be the harness, that fancy red show wagon over there and even a nice set of horseshoes worn by the Lucky Strike Heavy Horse Hitch. Everything but the horses, seeing as they've all gone to horse heaven!"

Dan was clearly enraged by this announcement. With ashes, words and spittle flying, he gave his brother a shove on the shoulder, knocking him back a step. No one intervened; they were caught up in the sale of the unusual lot.

Everyone knew of the old man's champion six-horse-hitch: the six well-matched dappled-grey Percherons. The Lucky Strike Team was legendary; they won money, ribbons and trophies galore in their heyday; they even took the Grand Championship at The Royal Winter Fair.

There never was a prettier sight than those immaculately groomed and be-ribboned muscular giants. Their polished harness ornaments shone brightly as the arena shook beneath their two dozen shod hooves, making anyone in the stands feel the sound thundering in their hearts. They were sad days when, one by one, the champions eventually died of ailments and old age, going on to what the old man hoped were greener pastures.

A confident woman in a leather coat and leather western hat and boots now stepped up in front of the auctioneer's perch. She was a heavy horse person herself and wanted to buy the whole kit and caboodle to set up her own six-horse-hitch.

"Ayyyydibba, ayyydibbadibbadibba…" The auctioneer was off to the races, generating more buzz for this collection, now that he was selling for the big bucks. His voice had competition, though.

"How dare you!" Dan demanded of his brother. "You know damn well that Dad always promised those horseshoes to me!"

Doctor Price said nought. He ducked his head and held up both hands in a stop sign. Luckily for the Doc, or so you'd-a thought, everyone, including Dan, swung around to see what was making a dramatic entrance now. It was a long trailer that teetered from side to side as the contents snorted and bashed and banged around inside.

Doc Price eased away from Dan and hailed the truck driver; he got in the passenger seat and motioned for the driver to go around to the back of the barn. Meanwhile, the leather-clad woman claimed her Lucky Strike six-horse-hitch prize and the auction moved on to selling the livestock. A few lads helped the leather woman move the harness and box of horseshoes over to the fancy show wagon.

The plaid Greek chorus spoke again.

"What the hell is Doc Price thinking?" asked the green plaid. "He's selling off his livestock and bringing more in?"

"Oh," said the red plaid, "he's onto this newfangled thing called rewilding."

"Rewilding? What in Sam's name is that?"

"Well, some folks figure that we screwed things up by farming. They want to go back to nature – something like that…"

"Is that so? Likely the same bunch that wants us to quit eating meat and start eating bugs!"

"Anyhow, the Doc wants to rescue wild mustangs; had a bunch delivered last week. They'll be unloading the new ones behind the barn now," explained the red plaid.

"Oh – look there! There they go, like the blazes!" said the brown plaid.

Everyone craned to see the mustangs tearing off in a streak. Sturdy horses – bays, chestnuts, a pinto - sped past some orphan oil wells that, in their day, had given Lucky Strike Farm its name. Even the kids and dogs fell quiet until the herd was out of sight over a rise in the land.

"Some folks call that horse meat," said the red plaid.

"Hey, Fred," the green plaid called to the overalls, "what would you rather eat - horsemeat or bugs?" Gags and guffaws followed.

The auction went through the livestock, farm machinery and some hay bales.

"I was hopin' to buy some straw," said the overalls.

"No chance," said the red plaid, who really was a fount of information. "Doc's startin' a business here teaching folks how to make straw bale houses!"

"Get *out*!" said the exasperated overalls.

Some people headed to their trucks. They needed to back up to the loading chute behind the barn, so as to wrestle their new livestock onto the trucks. The first person to drive behind the barn came running out, through the front door of the barn, surprising everyone. He was pale and breathless.

"Come quick," he said, "it's the Doc!"

Moving in one curious herd, everyone went through the barn or around the end of the barn to see what was what. They found the Doc, flat on his back in the dirt, rubber booted feet splayed apart. There was a nasty bruise turned black on the edge of his chin. Even the untrained eye could tell that the Doc's open eyes could act only as mirrors now to the blue sky and passing clouds.

A veterinarian stepped forward to examine the Doc's body. Gently, she lifted the white cambric shirt and peered underneath. The vet recoiled a little in surprise. Parting the sides of the thin shirt, she revealed that the Doc's pale body had a bruised imprint the shape of a horseshoe on his chest. The crowd recoiled too. The wound was in the middle of Doctor Price's chest and it had just broken the skin.

Police and medics soon arrived. No one was allowed to leave the premises. It was guessed that, in whatever manner the wound happened, it probably caused a fatal cardiac arrest.

"One of them wild horses must'a kicked him," ventured the red plaid.

"Nothin' of the kind," said the mustang trucker who had stayed on for the auction. "I was with him the whole time we unloaded.

None of them mustangs even came close to touching him. They couldn't wait to get away."

"Besides," said the brown plaid, now the wiser one: "Wild horses aren't shod. You can tell that wound wasn't just caused by a hoof. It was caused by a horseshoe – see there, you can make out the outline of the grooves along the sides and the imprint of the nail holes."

The police set about asking questions. No one present had witnessed what killed Doctor Price. There were, however, multiple witnesses to the ruckus with the Doc and his brother Dan. The police wanted to know what was the upshot of the argument. Well – it wasn't exactly an argument in the classic sense, between two people, the brown plaid conveyed. It was a quarrel - well – *between Dan.*

The leather woman, who'd bought the six-horse-hitch package, complete with the Lucky Strike Team's horseshoes, went over to the fancy show wagon and peered into the box beside the harnesses. She rummaged through the box and then shouted out a surprising announcement.

"There's only twenty-three horseshoes in this box I just bought!"

The collective grasped the import of this right away.

"Where is Dan?" they said to one another.

"His truck is still here," pointed out the brown plaid.

Now, the milling crowd and the police were looking for two things: Dan and the missing horseshoe.

It was pretty easy to guess that Dan had pilfered one of those horseshoes he was so mad about out of the box with no one noticing. Then - just think about how his beefy fist could have socked the Doc on the chin and knocked him out cold. Just imagine how Dan's heavy boot could press down on the stolen horseshoe, like a cookie cutter through dough, as he stood upon his hated brother's chest.

The red plaid finally found Dan in the hayloft of the barn. They walked out together, Dan roughly pulling his arm from the other man's grasp.

"What do you suppose he was he doing in there?" the red plaid asked the gawkers. "Smoking! In the barn! Again!"

Dan tried to get to his truck, but the police closed in on him.

"You need to come to the station with us for some questioning," they said.

"It's not a crime to have a cigarette in a barn," he snapped.

Blissfully unaware of human machinations, a crow circled overhead and looked down on the farmyard scene. It soared over the deep woods behind the barn, until it landed on the roof of a house a couple of concession roads away. Inside the house, a farrier was sitting down with his family for dinner and giving an account of his day. He was asked to shoe a skittish horse that a farmer had found on his land.

When this mighty horse wandered out of the woods that morning, the farmer spotted an opportunity to snag a means of free labour to haul logs out of the bush. He tempted the horse into a shed by leaving a trail of oats.

The farrier had one of the cross-tied horse's back feet lifted and resting between his chaps-covered knees. He made some headway with the shoeing, in spite of the brute's resistance. The windfall horse was feeling jazzed up on his high-octane oats, like a thoroughbred before a race.

He shifted his great weight onto the one leg the farrier was trying to hold up. Suddenly, the horse perked his ears up and lifted his head, as he heard something on the wind. He let out a shrill whinnying that shook his resonant body. It alarmed the two men.

"Let the crazy hellion go! No sense killing yourself over it," the farmer said, "I didn't pay for him anyway!"

One man slipped the halter off the frothing beast, while the other rolled back the sliding shed door. The horse bolted and galloped back to the woods from whence he came.

By evening, Lucky Strike Farm was empty of people and vehicles, save for one man and his little girl in the farm yard. They had gone home for supper and came back later when the farm yard would be quiet. Earlier in the day, the chickens had spread far and wide, evading capture. The girl and her dad set about catching the last of their new laying hens that the dad had bought at the auction.

The last one was clucking on the front doorstep of the barn. As they approached to scoop up the hen, the little girl said, "What's that up there?"

The dad's eyes followed her point to the top of the barn's doorframe.

"Oh," he said, "that's a superstition. If you hang up a horseshoe with the space at the top like that one is, it will hold good luck and keep your luck from running out."

The girl, her dad and their chickens left and Lucky Strike Farm fell silent in the dusk.

Out on the open prairie, a sorrel stallion raced to join the wild herd. His thick neck, broad hooves and well-rounded hindquarters betrayed a coupling of mustang and heavy horse. He summoned all of his energy, kicking up his heels into one big burst of power. The rising silver moon glinted off the only sign of submission he'd ever made: a single horseshoe.

Noah Brown

I'm a Problem Solver

I walk out the county jail with $30 to my name,
a dead phone, the keys to my car, and a BIC lighter.
The $30 came from Dad, generous old bastard,
right before the cops walked up to our car.
He handed me 3 crumpled up 10s and said,
"Don't say shit to them and you'll be out tomorrow.
I won't be out tomorrow though so hold on to this."
I was sitting in the back of the squad car,
with the cuffs around my wrists way too tight
so my hands fell asleep because the dick head cop
got all excited thinking he was arresting the next El Chapo,
a tow truck pulled up to add another problem. Dealing

with the towed car and however the fuck
I'm gonna pay for the court costs comes second
because if I'm gonna be miserable
I need a pack of cigarettes. Dear old dad
is gonna get out to no money and we can call it even.
I'm about to walk an hour from this jail
in the middle of bumfuck nowhere
to the closest gas station in slippers and pj pants. After

an hour of walking and sifting through made up
scenarios of what I'm gonna say to my father,
every scenario starts with me saying,
"I wish you told me when we got in the car
that Einstein was possessing you.
Really good idea to 'hide' crack in the cupholder,"
I've finally arrived at 7/11 with a hole in my slipper
and sweat staining the arm pits of my white tee.
Snatch two Gatorades and walk up to the counter.

Is that going to be all?
"Nah can I get a pack of Newport shorts?"

Okay your total is $10.43. Cash or card?
"Cash"

I pull out two of the tens from my pocket and hand it to him.
He whips out the marker on me and while he fucks off with that
I open up the Gatorade to take a sip but he looks up at me.
Sir these are counterfeit.
I roll my eyes. "What about this one?" Hand him the last bill.
Marker proves me an idiot.
He throws them in the garbage and tells me I can keep the
Gatorade.

I walk outside and dig through the cigarette butts in the ash tray,
find a half smoked Black & Mild with the wood chewed on,
and I thank God for whoever the knuckle dragging idiot was
that left this here for my chance to catch a breath and let it go.

Jenny Bates

Beethoven's Bust

You couldn't write like you do if you were any different, the page said. I live in what you would call, *unorganized territory.* The *law of the paw* — wild life rules here.

I grew up with the handsome bust of brooding Beethoven on the piano. Like a Deer I would sit bemused at the keys, gawking up with respect to his frown lines. He had a scanty smile, thundercloud soul, and he had to find out all about you. I loved him for it. I became a *performance major.* My favorite Symphony, Beethoven's *Pastorale.* It forever reminds me of tender buds, fragrant flowers and new green grass.

I've lived in the woods now for twenty-one years. I brought Beethoven's bust with me, set him down beneath fallen leaves, creeping mosses and briers. I wanted him to hear the same unending symphony of sound as I did. When we re-stained the house a few years ago, the workers found *him.* They asked who he was. I thought everyone would recognize Beethoven! even the passing beetle.

I had forgotten just where *he* rested. I try to find him again, but never have any luck. I think we both lost our destiny to this wild place. He lets me pass, then steps out into the trail and stares after me, smiling. I listen to the Sixth Symphony still as a Deer. The storm builds and shouts, throws stones to chase me away. *Beethoven could not have written like he did if he was any different.*

I smile, refreshed in tireless performance.

Jo Ann Hoffman

Fruit

A slow reveal:
ivory flesh undressed
by the blood-red peel
trailing from the fruit
in a single spiral strip.

I watch my daughter
watch her father
slip the knife
beneath the skin
and turn, turn, turn
the chubby prize
until its seamless coat
curls neatly
on the counter.

The two of them
munch sweet meat,
lick juice that
corkscrews down
their fingers
while the snake of skin
waits, coiled
near the kitchen sink.

My little girl
flicks bits of apple
from her lips
and reaches out
for more.
I think of Aphrodite
and her tempting trick,
of Eve who used her apple

to seduce,
and pure-as-Snow White
who never dreamed
what lay in wait
beneath the skin.

Joyce Schmid

Maui, With Grandchildren

I couldn't wait to see the teardrop butterfly again,
the angel fish, the rainbow butterfly,
the Spanish dancer throwing off its shell
and undulating in the surf.
I couldn't wait to hear the quiet underwater
with the only sound the rushing of my breath.
But now I'm tripping on my fins in sandy waves,
and when I put the breathing tube inside my mouth
I choke on it.

Everyone is kind—
they try to help me swim, they try to help me stand—
but I am falling, breathing sand, and realizing
I can't do this any more. The children swim away.
I see their snorkels poking through the waves,
the splashing of their feet.
I stand here dripping on the shore.

Look!
I'm throwing off my shell
and swimming deep among the clouds
of teardrop butterflies
and rainbow butterflies
and angel fish.
I'm breathing water like the air.

Sharon Louise Howard

Silence Breaking

Lauren stepped off the curb. Her right hand grasped the top of the mailbox in response to a flutter of lightheadedness. It lasted only a moment, but the ghost of it lingered. She hadn't a clue when she'd last checked the mail. Monday? Last week? A light September breeze stirred the whacked ends of her hair. Last night she'd taken the kitchen shears, and snipped off the long, amber curls Carson loved. She'd left the remains spread across the bathroom floor. Lauren felt exposed all the way back to the house.

She dropped the mail onto the side table next to the door, not even caring if there were any more cards. Always the damn cards—both best wishes and sympathy. Implying a paradox—that there was hope or that Carson was already gone.

There were also the voicemail messages, texts, and emails she had begun to ignore a couple days ago: her father, friends, neighbors, or Carson's patrol partner, all with the same question: Did she need anything?

To be left the fuck alone.

If one of those calls was the hospital, Lauren didn't want to know. She'd go in later, as always; talk to doctors, again. They would present her with the same choice to make, and Lauren would—as she had for the past week or more—have the same answer.

Maybe she'd wait for Sean to come home from school, and take him with her. The doctors wouldn't suggest such an action in front of a little boy.

In the kitchen, she moved across the tile floor quiet as a stalking cat while clearing the dinette table, putting the cereal in the pantry, the milk in the fridge, and the dirty dishes on the counter with the supper plates and pots she'd left the night before.

Lauren stood in front of the sink staring out the window at the wooden jungle gym Carson had built for Sean a couple years ago.

She snapped the blinds shut.

Then she washed the plates and bowls, lowering each to the sudsy water so as not to bang against the sink, or the faucet when she rinsed them. She eased the dishes into the drainboard rack, as if any sudden sound might release the unthinkable.

Decisions of late had been disasters. She couldn't be trusted to make another.

The macaroni-stuck pot from the night before would not come clean. Lauren scrubbed it with the sponge, and then the scraper—still stuck. She slammed the pot into the side of the porcelain sink. Silence shattered. The kitchen seemed too small to contain its breaking. With her hands still wet, she snatched the house key from the hook in the laundry room on her way out the side door. Rounding the garage, she paused in the driveway.

Her blue Neon sat there alone, like a puppy with its nose pressed against the garage door, wanting in. But that was not possible. Seven years ago, with the arrival of Sean imminent, they'd cleared out the second bedroom—up until then their makeshift storage room. Everything that could not be parted with, and would not fit anywhere else in the small house, went into the garage: old books, read and unread; boxes of photos to be sorted, some day; tennis rackets, golf clubs, bowling balls—the remains of sports taken up and given up over the years; Lauren's abandoned pottery wheel; boxes of high school and college yearbooks; Carson's baseball and swimming trophies.

Carson's things—they'd have to be gone through. How would she ever?

At the very least, she could back the car down the drive a bit. There was no need now to leave room for the Bronco.

Lauren turned right at the end of the driveway. The air hung heavy with the morning heat of a too-long, too-dry, and too-hot summer. Sunlight caressed her skin, like a warm hand on the back of her neck. Carson's hand. She missed that.

She never should have let him leave.

Lauren felt like a caged creature let loose—an anxious rabbit, alert, and a bit pink-eyed from lack of sleep. Too many insides for too long—the house, the car, the hospital, and especially the inside of her head. Lauren tried to make that exit as well. She focused on the sunlight upon her skin; the way the wilted, late-season tiger lilies drooped along the walkway in front of the corner house; and how the air held an invigorating scent recently released from a million chopped blades of grass. The drone of a lawn mower hummed from somewhere down the side street.

Lauren stopped at the corner. The cross street in front of her an obstacle.

Before her indecision could take hold, she stepped off the curb. The blast of a car horn shoved her back onto the sidewalk. Imagination took flight—to the smashed hulk of the Bronco.

A green leaf, then another and a third dropped from a nearby oak tree; the ground was strewn with them. They fell too early. There would be none left to carpet the ground in October, no crunch of crumbled colors the three of them had loved to trample through.

She could no more wish leaves back onto trees than she could wish back words.

Their last argument, about the dangers of Carson's job, had driven her so far over the edge she'd finally said aloud that whisper inside her head: *Take the desk job they'd offered. Please.*

Half an hour later, that request had morphed into a demand.

Carson had slammed his suitcase against the door jamb on his way out that night two months ago. The night she'd driven him away, right into the path of a sleep-deprived trucker.

Lauren closed her eyes. White light flashed behind her eyelids, the white of long corridors, and a maze of hallways all the same. Just follow the blue line, they'd told her.

But life didn't come with colored lines, and at the moment she couldn't decide which way to go.

Back inside, Lauren moved through the living room picking up the minefield of Sean's strewn toys—the action-figure heroes, the blocks that had been walls to hide behind, and the golf balls that had been bombs. She tossed them onto the lounge chair, and covered them with an afghan.

Lauren crossed the room. She sat down in the center of the sofa, slipped off her canvas shoes, and propped her feet on the coffee table. She stared at the afghan, rich in lavender and primrose. The last project her mother had worked on up until near the end, even on some of her better days during her last hospital stay. While another kind of needle pierced her body to deliver one final attack on the cancer within, she had finished the afghan.

"Keep your hands busy, it will calm your mind." Her mother's mantra.

Could it have been that easy? Lauren had tried knitting, but her stitches were always loose and uneven. She'd thought she could do what her mother had done for twenty-three years, waiting for Lauren's father to get home, first from far away battlefields, and later from his firehouse shifts. Perhaps it *hadn't* been that simple. There had been another way her mother kept her hands busy. The cigarettes—the ones she had lit anytime her hands where not otherwise occupied.

Lauren picked up the nail file she'd left on the coffee table the night before. After midnight, when sleep had still eluded her, she'd returned to the living room where she'd sat down to shape up her nails. But had soon given up out of weariness and apathy.

She awoke with a jolt. Her head rested against the couch-back cushions. Lauren tried to remember what she'd been doing. But she couldn't get past the dream. One as old as Sean. She would awaken terrified she had lost him, left him somewhere: in the car seat, in the shopping cart, out in the yard.

She sat up. Even now the dream left her feeling shaky and inadequate. She'd thought these dreams had finally gone away. Then about a year ago they returned—around the time Carson and his partner, Mike, walked in on a holdup at a convenience store. Mike had been shot in the shoulder before Carson had managed to take down the would-be robber.

Since then, in the dream, it was sometimes Carson she'd lost or left behind or could not find.

The first time she'd seen him, Carson had been five stories up on top of the Chem Building trying to talk a drunk freshman off the low wall that rimmed the roof. A crowd had gathered in the quad below. From one moment to the next, the two young men were in motion—the freshman leaning forward, and Carson making a desperate lunge to grab him around the waist to pull him back onto the roof, where they'd dropped out of sight behind the wall.

That was the moment Lauren had fallen in love with a hero.

The clock across the room chimed noon. She would need to take a shower before Sean got home. Instead, Lauren ended up back in the kitchen where she tossed the ruined pot into the trash, dried the dishes, and put them away. She pulled a rag and liquid cleaner from under the sink to wash off the counter, stove, and refrigerator in quick succession. She moved on to the smaller appliances. After that, she went to the bathroom, swept up the dregs of her amputated hair, and flushed them down the toilet.

By the time she finished, the ends of her hair against her neck were damp with sweat. Lauren leaned into the bathroom countertop. She gripped its edge. Her breath felt constricted, as if she had to inhale consciously. After two purposeful breaths, she raised her head. She continued to breathe deeply on her way back to the kitchen.

Lauren filled a glass pot with water and set it over the flame of the gas burner; then she took out a package of dry noodle soup mix. While waiting for the water to boil, she pulled a bread knife from a drawer, and set a fresh loaf of French bread on the cutting board. Her neighbor, Barb, had brought over the homemade loaf the day before.

Lauren had tried baking, too. *Keep your hands busy.* But she'd always managed to burn herself or the bread or both.

When the water began to boil, she stirred in the soup mix. Then Lauren put a slice of bread on a plate and took it, and the butter, to the dinette table to wait for the soup.

With slow, deliberate stokes she spread the butter on the bread.

Across the room the soup simmered, the small noodles drifted up, then back down in an endless cycle. Hypnotic. Like the snow globe, containing a unicorn with pink angel wings, her dad had bought her for her fourth birthday.

When Lauren had been stubborn about taking a nap, or would not go to sleep at night because she wanted to wait up for her daddy, her mother would hand her the snow globe. Lauren had turned it over again and again, until she'd drifted off to sleep as the snow descended one last time.

Lauren walked to the stove. She turned off the flame beneath the pot. The noodles settled—still and at rest.

Like a death. Like one final letting go.

Gordon Lindsey

War in Ukraine

The beginning of every war is like opening the door into a dark room.
One never knows what is hidden in the darkness.
    —Adolf Hitler

One night in Florida
a sinkhole swallowed a house,
its manicured lawn, swaying palms,
chandeliers, beds and their sleepers.

Rescuers stood at the brink
staring in amazement into the collapse.
Who knew that all these years
a jaw lay underground
biding its time,
waiting, waiting
to lay claim to the ordered world above it?

Black holes constitute parts of the universe.
We construct illusions, dogmas, myths, lies
to assure us massive gravity will not suck in the light.

In the end reality will have its way.
Against this rock our desperate lifeboats
crash, splinter, and sink.

Lillo Way

Infusions

*—plants and their extracts have been used for centuries
for the treatment of cancer. www.interchopen.com*

This one will rot too, of course, this spanking
new porch smelling of forest and pitch.

It will go the way of all wood in a rainy climate
but may outlast me. Me of the sagging blood tests

in sisterhood with the sagging porch,
torn and jaggered away in a truck bed.

You have hardly a natural killer cell in your body
they tell me, as if this were a bad thing.

They're bent on saving me by filling my veins
with wormwood—essence of absinthe, forgetting,

and Elizabethan slang for nonsense. If
this should fail, the would-be killer cells

will undergo some mistletoe, can you believe it?
Mistletoe, irresistible even to hardened criminals.

Rain silvers the new porch. Logs burn.
My left foot rests on the creature-eaten table,

pitted and pocked,
the work of worms.

Amy Marques

The baby died. The end.

In my memory he has *not* died yet.

My story starts in a small outpatient clinic where an unconscious toddler with a mop of blond hair lies on a cot many sizes too big, undressed, with an IV running much too slowly. In this story, I try everything I know in seconds that last an eternity. There are cold extremities, flimsy pulses, pale lips, and dry eyes. My story has all the right answers and a failed score.

There's a moment in every nightmare when the horror is so unbearable that you awaken—heart pounding, throat dry, lungs struggling for breath—relieved to find that you are safe. That is where the story stops, unfinished, only to begin again.

I was a young pediatric resident in need of extra income, so a slow shift in a small maternity ward sounded like a chance to get paid while catching up on much needed sleep. I don't remember who rushed into the doctor's lounge to ask for help. I don't remember why the clinic's pediatrician continued to see the fevers and diaper rashes that filled the waiting room instead of focusing on the sickest child. He was her patient. Not mine.

My only job was to snooze and wait in case some pregnant woman showed up. I had come prepared to help deliver babies and teach mothers how to breastfeed. The hospital where I spent most of my waking hours had a relentless stream of the severely ill and dramatically urgent. This shift was supposed to be a dream. I was looking forward to the change of pace.

I cried all the way home that night. I couldn't sleep.

The next day I worked in a daze: I saw other patients, smiled, took vitals, and wrote prescriptions. I told the story over and over to myself, my peers, my advisors. I examined every choice in search of wrong turns and missed opportunities, anything to suggest an explanation.

The toddler had been unresponsive. He had glassy eyes, floppy limbs, and sallow, sunken skin. He needed a new IV, but the equipment was inadequate for pediatrics, and I had to double check everything because the nurses were inexperienced in urgent care. We called every pediatric center in the area, but none were able to receive a transfer. Fluids, drugs, ventilation, compressions. Textbook sequence of events. Unfathomable outcome.

My mentors reassured me: *Given the resources at hand, you exceeded expectations. I couldn't have done better myself.*

I felt hollow and helpless. There *had* to be more to it than that: some lacking skill, some unspoken step, some elusive task.

Soon after, I was on shift at the university hospital when one of our chronic patients was transferred, yet again, to the ICU. He was only two years old, and he had an inoperable brain tumor. It was only a matter of time.

His mother sat on a backless bench in front of the elevators in the pediatric ward when I walked in from a lunch break. I had patients to see, prescriptions to write, a never-ending list of things to do. The usual. It could wait. I sat next to her. *What do you have there?*

Pictures. She had pictures of his two-year-old birthday party when he was still a round cheeked toddler who didn't yet know what was growing in his brain. Pictures of him playing with the family dog. Pictures of his grandmother holding an infant with a tiny afro and a toothless grin. She told me the stories of his short life. She laughed. We both cried. When she had gone through all the pictures, she stared at her hands as she told me of a life she'd only dreamt of but knew she would never see: his next birthday, his first day of school, his first girlfriend, his first child.

I remember the night he died. I sat with his mother and we watched his chest rise and fall. Shallow. Erratic. Then, finally, not at all. We held our breath as the heart monitor tripped and staggered, pausing, then starting again, slower and slower until the beeping pattern came to a halt. The hush surrounded us, and we hardly breathed, wondering if that was the last time. It was. He was gone. We had done what we could. It wasn't enough.

I hugged his mother. The whole team cried together: nurses, social workers, doctors, and family. Everyone knew what to do. That was part of the job: the aftermath, the reminiscing, the relief.

That day I began to understand how little I had known. We are all haunted by the faces of those we could not save. We make our peace with that. And we honor their death.

When a little boy died in a clinic where I wasn't even the pediatrician on call, I told myself *my* story over and over: every symptom, every drug, every move. But it wasn't my story. It was his.

I didn't sit with his parents in their pain or give them a chance to say goodbye. I never learned their pet name for him or how they rocked him to sleep. I don't remember telling them they had done all they could, and it wasn't their fault. I don't know how they grieved, who they blamed or what they understood. I don't know if their marriage survived, if they had other children, or if they ever spoke his name.

I was younger then. I knew so much. I knew nothing. To this day, I doubt we could have changed the course of the disease. But I do know that I failed that day. It was a failure in kindness, not in medicine.

This is all I know of their story: A young couple had a child. The toddler got sick. They went to the hospital. Their boy lost consciousness. He was whooshed inside. The baby died.

It was not the end.

Joyce Schmid

Zooming

My father lived so far away,
we rarely saw each other
and he used to say, *Someday*
someone will make a television-phone
that shows our faces.

I don't see him in dreams.
He visits me in sound
when someone plays a violin.
But it has happened as he said.
My children are a mini-series on a screen,
their children opening like lilacs
seen through safety-glass, a sliding door
that doesn't slide. They see me on tv,
they take it in their stride,

love subject to the law of inverse squares,
like gravity, like light.

Hunt Smith

Day Drinking

We drank like dogs on a hot summer day. Slurping up the gin, rum, and whisky without any regard for consequences. It was how we lived. It was how we were expected to live, young and without care for decency. It took a certain amount of courage to drink so much, as you had to blatantly disregard friendships and financial security, as both became disposable after ingesting enough booze.

"Another round," John called out to the waiter.

"Oh, can't we go off and do something," Emily said. "All we do is sit around and drink."

"What did you have in mind?" I asked.

"Oh, I don't know. Anything," Emily replied.

"Maybe you'll be able to think of something after another round," John suggested, motioning to the waiter who had stalled at Emily's request.

It was the five of us back then. Well, really three. John, Emily, and I tolerated the overly affectionate couple.

"Where did William and Dee go?" Emily asked.

"They probably found a bathroom somewhere," I suggested.

The waiter brought out our drinks. They were strong, just as we had liked them.

"Oh, let's go do something," Emily protested.

"What can be better than this?" John asked.

We sat outside in a dingy alleyway that was modeled to look like a Parisian street, but the decorators had failed remarkably. The street was damp and sticky, despite the fact that it had not rained in over two weeks. But to drunken tourist it was like stepping into another world, another time.

As Nashville natives, we knew better, but the drinks were cheap, and the people watching was better than any reality TV show.

"Let's go to the Ashton! I love a rooftop bar," Emily said.

"And pay double for the same drink that I can get here," I protested.

"It's not about the drinks. It's about the location!"

"And what's so bad about this location?" John asked.

"It's gross and everyone that passes by is wearing a cowboy hat."

"That's the fun of it!" I suggested.

"No, Blake. Let's please go to the Ashton," Emily said.

"I can't afford the Ashton," I said.

"I can pay for your drinks," John offered.

"I'm not letting another man pay for my drinks."

"C'mon Blake! I'm sure that I can find you a girl at the Ashton," Emily said.

"Why can't you find me a girl here?"

"I can find you alley trash here, but I can find you a lady at the Ashton."

"Maybe he doesn't want a lady," John joked. "Based on his track record, a lady is not quite his type."

"Ok, one more drink here, and then I can afford the Ashton," I said.

Emily goaded me into chugging my drink. I'm not sure what it is about women, but they always want to be on the move. They could never find a place that they deemed nice enough to sit and drink for a while. For me, the location did not matter as much as the company. The most beautiful place in the world could be ruined by a smug asshole.

We called an uber to take us to the Ashton. Ubers were fun when you were drunk, and we were good and drunk. We wanted to learn everything we could about our driver, but he did not return the enthusiasm, as he pretended that he couldn't hear us. He had the radio turned to a Christian rock station and gave us disapproving looks at every available opportunity.

We were quiet at first, until Emily chimed in, "Could you change the station?"

The balding old man scowled and turned the volume up. John and I snickered in the background. Emily began to sing along with the radio in response. She knew all the words from growing up in the church, but she no longer believed them. She told me once that her overly conservative parents beat the Christianity out of her. I told her that she was better than me: she at least had the courage to take a side.

The Uber driver did not appreciate Emily's worship and turned off the radio. We rode in silence for the next few minutes until reaching our destination.

"You just fucked up your Uber rating," I joked as we exited the car.

"Ah, whatever," Emily replied.

We entered the Ashton hotel. It was a nice hotel, fancy without being gaudy. It stood as a testament to Nashville's entrance into the one of the elite cities. While the boot barns and honky-tonks still littered Broadway, new Hotels made of sparkling glass began to dominate the skyline. And so, it became fashionable to drink at an overpriced rooftop bar. The higher the bar, the more expensive the drinks, and the Ashton towered over the entire city.

"William texted me," John said. "They want to know where we went."

"Are they gonna meet up with us?" Emily asked.

"I dunno. William's pissed that we left them."

"That's what they get for not being able to keep their hands off each other," I said.

"Tell them that they have to come," Emily said.

"He said that the Ashton is too expensive," John said.

"A little late for that," I said.

"Fuck 'em" John said.

"No, tell them to come!"

"They are just gonna ditch us anyway," I said.

"They're coming," John said.

"Good," Emily said.

As we rode up the elevator, my legs began to sway. The elevator jostled me, as it sped up to the top floor. I took a wide stance to steady myself. John and Emily laughed, but I remained focused on staying upright. The doors opened and I took a deep breath and walked off. I had gotten to the point where I became extremely aware of how drunk I was. I needed to sit down. I needed to have another drink.

The hallway opened up to a large bar area with a smattering of chairs surrounding a large oval bar, stocked with expensive liquors. Past the bar was an open patio that overlooked the city. We found a seat that had enough shade to remain pleasant while still giving the thrill of outdoor drinking.

The waitress came up, and I ordered a gin and tonic, John a bourbon, and Emily an alcoholic slushy.

"Is that why you wanted to come here?" I asked. "For the slushy."

"Don't give me grief. They're good."

"They better be, for the price," I said. Behind me a group of tourists were drinking champagne out of a beer bong.

"You must admit," she said. "It has a much better view than the alleyway. It's more glamorous."

"Why do we need glamor?" I asked.

"It's good to have some glamor," John said.

"I can do without it."

"The girls are more attractive," Emily said.

"The girls come here to take pictures, not to have fun."

"And you need a girl that wants to have fun?" John asked.

"Doesn't everyone," I said.

"I don't," Emily joked.

"But *you* like to have fun," I offered.

"Sure," she said.

The drinks came out garnished with unnecessary fruit and accessories. They were weak and unsatisfying. I missed the guttural sting of the cheap drinks in an alley, but that was not glamorous. Girls wanted the atmosphere to intoxicate them as much as the drinks, and I wanted to follow the girls.

However, it was beautiful. The sunlight glanced off of the glass buildings and onto Emily's bright yellow hair, which absorbed the rays of sunlight and became its own light source. She smiled as she drank her slushy and puckered when it gave her a brain freeze.

"We could've just brought some booze to Sonic," I joked.

"What's the fun in that?" Emily asked.

"It's frugal," I suggested.

"And being frugal is fun?" she asked.

"It can be."

John's head was swiveling around the table, as he tried to get a glance at each individual girl, sizing them up by how open they may be to a new adventure.

"What do you think about her?" John asked.

"Who?"

"Her!" He said pointing me in the direction of a tall slender brunette. She was swaying a little but still seemed to have a firm grasp on reality. She had a small tattoo at the end of her forearm, suggesting that she was conservatively wild.

"She's cute." Emily said.

"Yeah, but you are going to have to extricate her from her friends."

"I'll just lightly bump into her."

"She'll fall," I said.

"No, I'll be super graceful about it."

"You're not a graceful person," Emily laughed.

"I'll be careful."

"You better try something else," I said.

"There are only four of them," he said. "Come with me, Blake."

"I don't wanna leave Emily."

"She'll be fine."

"Let's just wait William and Dee. Then I'll go with you."

"They might be gone by then. Plus, who knows if they will even show up," he said.

"Go, I'll be fine. Watching you two strike out is the only entertainment I need."

I sighed and dove back into my drink. I was in no mood to listen to boring girls talk about their boring lives, and these girls looked cute enough that they never had to be interesting.

"Can't we just drink?" I asked.

"Pussy," John exclaimed.

Emily smirked and went back to drinking. She enjoyed watching us fail. She had seen us stumble up to countless girls, and we always ended up hobbling back alone.

"So, what we just go up and say hi?" I asked.

"Sure," John said. No matter how many times he got rejected, he always exuded a degree of confidence that I was never able to match.

I downed my drink and got up, "Order me another," I told Emily. "We won't be long."

John scowled and marched me over to the pack of girls who were leaning against the side railing. Their conversation sounded like a high-pitched buzz, as they talked over constantly in hopes of making some useless point.

"Hey," John said to them. I hid behind John, as I didn't want to be fully a part of the train wreck.

"Hi," the brunette said coldly before turning back to her friends.

"My name is John, and this is Blake."

"Cool," she said.

I began to laugh uncomfortably and walk away. "This is typically the part where you say your name," John said.

"Ok," she responded.

I thought that would be the end of it, but John was so stubborn that he just sat and waited, forcing the girl into a response. I looked at Emily who was mindlessly drinking her slushy. My drink had arrived. I longed to turn back to the safety of the table.

"Um… my name is Anna, and this is Sarah, Lyton, and Amber," she said.

"Nice to meet you," John said, trying to laugh off the awkward introduction. "Could we buy you a drink?"

"Knock it off, John," I scoffed.

"No, y'all can buy us a drink," one of the girls protested.

"I don't wanna buy you a drink," I protested.

"Ok, then," one of the girls said with the chagrin of entitled disappointment.

"Don't listen to him," John said to the girls. "We'll buy a few drinks and get to know each other."

"That's one fucking expensive conversation," I was becoming slightly belligerent, but I contained myself. "Plus, my drink is over there." I pointed over to my gin in tonic. As I glanced over, I saw the ice saturating the gin, zapping away its bite. Emily waved.

"Shots!" John proclaimed. "Let's get some shots. Blake shots?"

I rolled my eyes and walked away. I overhead John say: "We can do shots without him," and a slight woo from the bland, stereotypical girls.

"You struck out," Emily laughed.

"I think John knew that I'd be an asshole."

We both laughed. I took a long, slow sip of my drink, relishing the taste of good tonic, fresh unlike the plastic bottled stuff they give out at cheap places.

"Can I ask you something?"

"I hate when people ask that," I said.

Emily went ahead without my permission: "Why don't you like those girls?"

I crossed my arms and sat back in my chair. I took a sip to either think or stall, I'm not sure which.

"Aren't they pretty enough?" she asked.

I washed the gin around my mouth, crunching the ice between my teeth. "Yeah, they're hot," I laughed.

"So?" she asked.

"So what?"

"So, why did you leave John stranded?"

"Because they are so fucking boring that by the time that I got drunk enough to talk to them, my dick wouldn't work." I thought that would be the end of it.

"So, how is John able to talk to them?"

"Because John is a bore too. Just a little bit less so. I mean look at them," I said pointing at John continuing to prattle on. "They are probably talking about their favorite show to binge on Netflix. You shouldn't be proud that you watched three seasons of the Office in one weekend. Have some shame for fuck's sake."

"So, we should talk about Plato or Aristotle?" Emily joked.

"Or the weather."

"It is nice out."

"Very," I said, glancing deeper into her eyes. They were deep blue, but not necessarily the prettiest shade of blue. It was almost as if God had gotten distracted and not put enough color in them. They were dulled but distinct.

"Well. you see, John," Emily said in a mocking voice. "I'm a three wing four."

"So interesting. I think I'm a seven, but that is just what people tell me," I played along with the ruse.

"Oh, you don't know! You have to know! How can't you know your enneagram!" We both laughed.

"You make me laugh," I said. "Not a lot of people can make me laugh."

We sat in a contemplative silence, knowing what we were both thinking and trying not to think it.

"Well look who it is!" I exclaimed breaking the tension. "How was fucking?"

"Oh, shut up!" Dee said.

"Where's the menu?" William asked.

"QR Code," Emily said.

"Fuck these things," William said.

Emily and I both laughed, not at William, but at what we had just avoided. Everything suddenly felt lighter, not necessarily better but just less burdensome: like a walk around the block instead of a hike in the woods.

"Why'd we come here," William said, as he looked at the prices.

"Emily wanted a change in scenery."

"I was tired of looking sewage run down that filthy alley."

"Ooooh, what is that drink?" Dee asked.

"Where's John?" William asked.

"Currently throwing away money in hopes of getting laid," I said.

"Why doesn't he just skip the middleman?" William joked.

"Shut up," Dee said, slapping him on the shoulder lightly.

"Let's go somewhere to get drunk!" William suggested, playing off Dee's rebuke.

"Why not here?" Dee asked.

"You don't get drunk in a place like this," I said.

"Oh… and why not?" Emily asked, leaning forward as if to interrogate me.

"Here," William said, "they kick drunks out."

"And you want to get *that* drunk tonight?" Emily said, directing the question at me.

"I always want to get that drunk," I said in a soft tone. After I said it, I couldn't decide if it was charming or sad, but it was true.

Despite Williams protestations, Emily ordered a slushy for herself, and he ordered a bourbon. He would do anything for her, but he would always make a fuss about doing it. I often wondered if she would reciprocate, how far she would go to make John happy. Not very far I supposed. I don't know if that was an indictment on her or rather a sign that I distrusted all women, no matter their character.

"He's still alive," Emily said. She looked over her shoulder and took a glanced at John's escapades. Dee took a less subtle approach.

"You jealous, Blake?" Emily asked.

"Of what?" I asked and Emily moved her eyes to direct my gaze at John moving ever closer to the tall brunette. "I told you, she's not my type."

"Ahh, right she's too boring," Emily said.

"She doesn't look boring," Dee said, scanning up and down her body. William did the same. Dee, again, slapped William.

"I'm not going to devote several hours of my life for 30 minutes of pleasure," I said.

"I'm guessing it's more like 30 seconds," Emily said with a wry smile.

"Even more reason," I said, shirking off the insult.

"I don't know, Blake, it looks like things are going pretty well. It might not take as long as you think," William said.

"Please, she'll end up dragging him to some shitty bar to hear some shitty band," I said.

"I thought you loved shitty bars," Emily said.

"I love cheap, shitty bars. There's a difference."

"I think you're just a pussy," William said.

I scoffed at William's remark. There was really no proper response to this allegation other than get up and go talk to the group of girls, which would be far more painful than the insult.

"Be easy on him. He'll come out of his shell one of these days," Emily said. I knew that she was mocking me, but she seemed almost genuine, as if she truly believed that I was not now what I might someday be. That is, she believed that there would be some day in the future where I don't immediately become an introverted asshole at the sight of pretty girls. However, I felt that I had developed as far as I would in life, and my personability was now on a long crescendo toward complete isolationism.

"Poor boy never learned how to talk to girls," Dee said.

"Fuck y'all," I said. I took a long slow sip of my now watery beverage, as Emily, Dee and William laughed at their wit. "Maybe, I just have a different approach than John."

"And what approach would that be?" Emily asked.

I paused and looked down at the floor as if I was about to say something really deep and meaningful, but in reality, I was buying time to think of an answer. "Sure, I could buy a slag a drink and hope that buys me a lay. It might work, or I might be out 200 hundred dollars with my dick in my hand at the end of the night."

"But you gotta take risks in order to meet someone, to see if there is a spark," Emily said.

"The closest thing I would get to a spark with that girl is a shotgun wedding."

"So, you know *that* quick?" Emily asked.

"Of course. Didn't y'all" I asked William and Dee, knowing that they would support my claim.

"So, when you met me… were there…sparks?"

"There could've been," I said. "If you weren't dating that limp dick, Justin."

"Fuck you," Emily said. "He was a nice guy."

Dee nodded along.

"He was an ass and had the face of one, too," I said.

"Ok, he wasn't my best."

"*Your best*," I said. "C'mon Emily. You couldn't have a five-minute conversation with the guy without wanting to blow your own brains out."

"He wasn't that bad," Dee said.

"The guy was a *Formula one* enthusiast from Birmingham, Alabama!"

"So, the fact that I dated a guy like Justin made you think of me the same way you think of those girls over there."

"No, you're not boring," I said. "You just have a boring taste in men."

"What if I think that you're a little boring?" Emily asked.

"Let's get another drink," I said.

My drink had become diluted to the point where it was just water, and Emily's slushy had melted into a concoction of sludge and juices that no longer looked appetizing. She finished it anyway.

Emily walked to the bar together. It was an awkward few steps as we detached from William and Dee. Everything felt more comfortable at the bar.
"You really think I'm boring?" I asked.

Before she had a chance to answer, John joined us at the bar. He acted calm but it still seemed like he was in a rush.

"Anna and her friends wanna go to Broadway, so--"

"Anna?" I asked in jest.

"The girl… from over there," John said. "Fuck you. You know who she is."

"And she wants to go to Broadway?" I said, looking at Emily.

"Yeah, do y'all wanna come?" John asked.

"No," Emily said decisively.

That was the last we saw of John for the night, as he hurriedly followed the gaggle of girls from one tourist trap to the next.

"I should've put money on it," I said after John left.

Emily laughed, as we watched John hobble out of the bar with his gaggle of girls. He was so enthusiastic and without reproach. I looked at Emily and smiled. She smiled too.

"You think it will work out?" Emily asked.

"Nah, things usually don't," I said.

"Yeah, things don't usually work out," Emily said.

We ordered our drinks and continued drinking, as we had in the past. We drank until they wouldn't let us drink anymore, and then we went home to drink some more.

Earl Carlton Huband

Thinking of "Love in Infant Monkeys"
from *An Introduction to Psychology*

"Love, remember that monkey, the one
on the cover of that monograph —
University of Wisconsin
I think it was, back in the Sixties —

"clinging to a wire apparatus
covered with terry cloth, the nipple
of a bottle of milk protruding,
the body caught in the wire, hanging . . . ?

"Sometimes, when we make love, and I feel
I am not here with you, you with me,
I go back to that monkey, clinging."

John Haugh

Ghost of a 1960 Ford F-100

I am fifteen on our farm, where foreman Joe calls the red truck, "Power."
Battered fifties curves, Ghostbuster headlights & preschooler paint job.
The beast's massive Y-block engine pushes us through water up and over
its hood. Tractors churn, useless until Power and the heavy chain arrive.

An unseasonable storm brings black early. Herefords bolt
through the wrong fence. Three of us cram beast's cab to sortie.
Maybe it's a spark plug or the Ford-O-Matic transmission?
We move lurch-shudder-pause, eight smooth feet, then rough.

Joe never swears, but grumbles before a newborn's last breath,
four in the morning after a bad birth. In beast's cab, Joe now
grumbles. Rain curtains charge like line-dancing infantrymen.
Lightning, eyeblink-fast liquid-flows down a pine twelve feet away.

Four chambers in my heart, like Ford-O-matic spark plugs.
I live lurch-shudder-pause. I need to settle up with fifteen
family ghosts. Smooth my spirit-engine spark plugs
or take a damned long walk home in the cold-wet
to a sister who has not spoken to me in seven years.

Emma Grace Myers

Bleecker Street

One.

I watch a nurse climb onto a chair in the second floor waiting room. An emergency light attached to a fire alarm that does not sound has been flashing, brightly, annoyingly, incessantly, since I got up here 20 minutes ago. The kind of flashing that those 50s "duck and cover" videos implied was the sign of an atomic bomb being dropped near you. But less dire. Just an irritant. She tapes a glove box over the light. You can still see it flashing around the edges.

I got separated from my boyfriend right away. So I'm up here alone, twiddling my thumbs and texting him. I take comfort in knowing he's just downstairs until he tells me that he's actually a few blocks away. He left the first-floor waiting room to go putz around Bleecker Street. He tells me he's getting coffee and avocado toast. I tell him I'm jealous, which is true: partially because I didn't get to eat anything before we left my apartment early this morning, for fear of eliminating the option to go under, and partially jealous of the food itself, the thing currently taking his attention. Before I took the elevator to the second floor, I gave them his number to be my emergency contact.

An ultrasound tech calls my name. I don't know how far along I am, so I have to get one to determine my options. Fine.

"Do you want to know the sex of the baby?"

No.

"Do you want to know if there are multiples? Twins, or more?"

No.

"Do you want to hear the heartbeat?"

No.

"Do you want to see the sonogram?"

No.

"Do you want to know exactly how far along you are?"

...Yes. (I'm just curious.)

7 weeks and 6 days.

Two.

Back in the waiting room, I count back in my calendar.

Turns out I got pregnant the night of Adam's wedding — send.

That's hilarious. I can't wait to tell him

Lol.

I tongue the vein on the inside of my cheek. We started Officially Dating the weekend of that wedding. *And* he put a goddamn baby in me. Talk about making it official.

The edges of the glove box taped to the wall still flash. The building is not on fire. The building just feels like it might be. Not to worry. Even as I remember the sound of my school's fire alarm.

When we had fire drills in high school, we would stand in the parking lot next to the teachers' cars. There was one Special Ed teacher who had a bumper sticker on the back of his that said, "Abortion stops a beating heart," with an artist's crude rendering of a fetus in utero. His car that he drove to work at a public school. I think about how that shouldn't have been allowed. I think about how that teacher really respected me as of the last time I saw him, and how he might not anymore if he knew where I was right now. Like that matters.

Three.

I sit in a chair in a small beige office next to a woman at a computer and I brace myself for judgment. She rattles through questions.

"Were you using protection?"

No.

I'm ready for a "why not?" Or at least a side-eye. I'm stupid, and I was very reckless in not using protection. I'm not even on birth control. Clearly.

I'm ready to explain that when I was a young teenager, I went to multiple doctors for multiple years, getting ultrasounds and getting my blood drawn and tested constantly to figure out why my period was so irregular, but nothing was ever wrong, huh, that's so weird, you're totally healthy, but then it came up with an endocrinologist when I was fifteen that infertility runs in my family on my dad's side, which I never knew, and oh maybe that's it, and you shouldn't worry because there's all this technology now, so chances are, even if that is the issue, you will probably still be able to have your own children, and, like, what do you even do with that information when you're a fifteen-year-old virgin, right?

You internalize it and, from when you become sexually active, have protected sex always, because you are cautious by default, until your college boyfriend convinces you to skip the condom once when you both don't have one, and nothing ever happens. So then, after that, when you have longer term partners, you're more lax about the protection of it all, and you hardly ever consider that anything even could happen. And you have no issues for, like, two and a half years with that course of action.

Because you're probably infertile, right? **_WRONG._**

But no judgment ever comes from the woman at the computer in the small beige office. She just keeps going through the questionnaire, kindly and understandingly. I appreciate that.

If nothing else, at least now I know, for sure, that I'm not infertile, and I guess that's something. Jury's out on whether that's a good or bad something. What if this is just a fluke, you know? What if I am only able to get pregnant once, ever, and it just so happens to be when I'm 22, making minimum wage, two months into a relationship that, despite my best efforts, I do not feel especially confident or comfortable in? Stuck in a situation where, yeah, of course, abortion is the obvious and, frankly, only option? I bury that thought — I already got misty about it briefly on the day I found out, and I don't want to do that again right now, or ever.

No, I do not want counseling (I want to get out of here as soon as possible and be done with this).

Yes, people support me in my decision. My boyfriend and my mom (even though I probably wouldn't have told her if I wasn't still on her insurance).

Yes, the surgical option is the preference (I would much rather this experience last eight minutes than two days).

Yes, I want to go under. All the way. Please knock me the fuck out. You can just hit me over the head with a big cartoon hammer, if that's easier. Whatever it takes.

Four.

I woke up on a Monday feeling excessively tired. But I just assumed it was a regular I-don't-want-to-go-to-work tired. I showered, felt a little better, and left my apartment for my midtown office building.

Later, I sat at my desk eating lunch and was hit with a very intense wave of nausea. I thought I might throw up right there, but it passed. It was the end of October. I started kicking myself for not getting the flu shot sooner. I had been saying that I needed to go get it but never got around to it, and now I was suffering the consequences. Stupid. Eye roll. Sigh.

In the late afternoon, I got a headache so terrible I couldn't focus my eyes on my computer screen. I left work right at six and went home, riding the subway with my eyes closed and my head leaned up against the wall of the train. The 1 felt especially crowded and rattly.

Heading up the stairs of my six-floor walkup, I started feeling nauseous again, more seriously this time. I ran up the remaining three flights as my mouth filled with saliva. I made it into my apartment just in time to barely throw up into the toilet, then dry-heaved for a few minutes. When it passed, I felt better. Still weird, but better. I wondered if I ate something bad. I wondered if the flu shot was still effective even if you were already feeling it coming on. I wondered how much work I would have to miss.

I started making dinner and texted my boyfriend about how I wasn't feeling well. About how mad I was at myself for procrastinating getting a flu shot when I could have just swung by a pharmacy and gotten it anytime. What an idiot! I told him my symptoms.

are you pregnant?

I chuckled to myself. *No, that's impossible* — send.

okay

We moved on. We talked about something else.

When I woke up the next day, I felt less sick, but I still felt weird. I'd had mono, the flu, food poisoning, strep throat, stomach bugs… This didn't feel like any of that. I still went to work.

I pushed through the morning, but by lunchtime, I couldn't focus on anything except how weird I felt. *"are you pregnant?"* I told a coworker I was going to grab lunch and left my Times Square office building to go to the Walgreens across the way. I bought a package of 2 ClearBlue Digital Pregnancy Tests — the kind that tell you, point-blank, in words, Pregnant or Not Pregnant. They were expensive.

I went back up to the 37th floor and went straight to the bathroom, the last stall. I took a test and waited. And then I went back to my desk. My boyfriend texted me.

how are you feeling?

Bad.

do u want me to buy a preg test and bring it over later?

Way ahead of you

did you take it?

Yes

what did it say?!

Five.

The soonest available appointment we could both go to and take off the least amount of work possible was today: Saturday, November 10th, 2018, 8:30am. I count back in my calendar to that day that we scheduled it, the day after I started feeling sick.

I was just over six weeks along. 11 days ago.

The tape has given way on one side of the glove box covering the emergency light. The box hangs limply to the side as the light blindingly flashes in the room again. A nurse gets on a chair to fix it. A futile effort, if you ask me.

They call my name. I text my boyfriend downstairs and tell him I'm going in, should be out within a half hour.

ok! i care about you deeply!

He does not tell me he loves me because he doesn't, and he won't.

Six.

As I disrobe to put on a hospital gown, I regret my choice to wear sneakers without socks. On my way into the operating room (is that what they call it?), I caught a glimpse of the stirrups at the end of the table, and it occurred to me that, duh, I'm going to have my disgusting, stinky, sweaty, sockless feet directly in this woman's face. I want to preemptively apologize to her but also don't want to draw attention to it (as if she's not going to notice).

I draw back the curtain in my newly donned gown to reveal three women: the doctor, the anesthesiologist, and another featured player whose job I am unsure of. The doctor smiles at me and kindly asks if I want her to write me a prescription for birth control pills.

Yes please yes thank you yes.

I get up onto the table, put my feet in the stirrups, and stare at the tiled ceiling. The doctor tells me, in a quiet and sweet voice, that

I will wake up in the recovery room within 15 minutes. I nod and wait for the anesthesia to kick in, but instead I hear her voice again.

"Sorry, could you just move your hips closer to the edge of the table, towards me?"

I awkwardly shimmy down a little farther until I feel like I'm on the edge of falling off. I rely heavily on the stirrups to keep myself on the table. I wonder if this has made the effect of my feet more terrible, somehow. Did I take a shower this morning? Should I have? Oh God, am I gross?

"Perfect, thank you."

Seven.

I come to, sitting in a chair in a line of chairs. There's a small cup of apple juice and a package of graham crackers next to me. I notice that the girl to my right has saltines, and suddenly I feel like I won a prize.

I survey the room: women, girls, all types of recently pregnant people sit in chairs, recovering. Some are escorted out as others are brought in on gurneys. Crackers, juice, water, pamphlets, goodbye. I feel like I am on the outside looking in until a woman kneels next to me and asks how I'm feeling. Right — I'm here, too.

She tells me I got a good laugh from the folks who brought me in here, because as I was first waking up, someone asked me if I was okay. I wasn't conscious enough yet to speak, but I did flash an emphatic thumbs-up, which everyone thought was very funny. I tell her I don't remember that happening, but that sounds like me. I notice that at this moment that I feel more like myself than I have in months. More like I'm in my own body again. Ain't that something.

She runs through her spiel and I only catch pieces of it. Cramping in a few days, sure, potential lemon-sized clots, okay, birth control prescription, got it, you can have sex again whenever you're comfortable, understood. I feel too tired to listen attentively, but I try to make it seem like I am. I would like to go home and lay down.

Eventually, I get up and gather my things from the locker I stowed them in. I take the elevator back down and meet my boyfriend in the first floor waiting room. We walk out onto Bleecker Street. He asks me if I want to go get food, go get coffee, go do something. I tell him I would like to go home and lay down. He calls an Uber. I stare at the second floor windows of the building, trying to see if I can still see the emergency light flashing until I remember it was covered. I bet it's still flashing under the box. But it's too sunny out to see much of anything anyways. My eyes are tired and have not yet adjusted.

In the backseat of the Uber, I ask my boyfriend to text my mom that I'm okay. He pulls out his phone to do so, referencing the number I gave him this morning. He does not save her contact.

We ride up the east side back to my apartment. I lean my head back on the headrest. It feels heavy, like my neck can hardly bear its weight. The sun glints brightly off the East River. I close my eyes to block the light but I can still kind of see it through my eyelids.

Soon, we will get back to my apartment and say hello to my roommates, who do not know where we were this morning. They won't ask, and that will be fine. I will text the one friend who I told about this, because she had also had an abortion before, and I will let her know I'm okay. I'll answer a text from my mom.

My boyfriend and I will go to the grocery store and buy some stuff to eat, and he will carry everything back so I don't have to. I will cook for both of us.

We will watch the Great British Bake-Off for the rest of our Saturday off together.

We will have sex later that night, and afterwards he will jokingly remark, "I love abortion sex," and I will cry.

I will go back to work on Monday, but have to call out on Tuesday and Wednesday because the cramping I am experiencing as my body realizes it is no longer pregnant and adjusts accordingly will make it too painful to stand up.

Over the next several weeks, I will tell some of my friends what happened. I will be very blasé about it, in an effort to prevent further questioning. I will feel less and less like myself, for reasons both related and unrelated to my abortion.

In January, to my surprise, a bill for $900 will arrive at my parents' house. Despite the hours I spent on the phone with Empire Blue Cross prior to the procedure to confirm that both the doctor and facility would be covered in full. Despite humiliatingly and tearily admitting to my mother that I got pregnant in hopes of avoiding this exact situation. My mom will be forced to tell my father about the abortion I had two months ago. He, like my mom was, will be supportive, kind, and gentle, and I will feel guilty about not telling him in the first place. He will tell me he gets it. I will feel like my parents really have my back. I will fight the bill and prevail.

In the following months, various states will present and pass six-week and heartbeat abortion bills. I will read article upon article upon article about the bans and think almost incessantly about how if I lived in any of these states, I would still be pregnant, and I would have to have a baby, and my life would be completely different. I will scroll all the way to the bottom of each article and read the comments, where, among any number of expected anti-abortion zealots, I will also find people saying things like, "No exceptions for rape or incest?! This is crazy!" I will read take upon take upon take about the need for abortion access in the wake of tragedies. I will read nothing about the need for abortion access in the wake of simply unwanted pregnancies. I will let the information and discourse wash over me, consume me, eat me from the inside, but I will never talk to anybody about it.

In April, my boyfriend will break up with me and I will be devastated, for reasons both related and unrelated to my abortion.

After the breakup, I will feel like such a shell of myself that I will start going to therapy. After weeks of looking, I will finally find someone who takes my insurance and has availability that works with my job. I will talk about how sad I am about the relationship, and about how I ignored my feelings about my abortion for six months. I will have several moments where I feel very judged by this therapist, but will shake it off, assuming it's just me — I am just uncomfortable with the vulnerability associated with being honest about your feelings. After a few months of continued talking about it, she will imply that the reason I am sad about the abortion is because I feel guilty about killing a baby. I will cry and tell her that's not fair. I will continue to see her for four more months after that because I feel I have no other options, and I wager that some therapy is better than none. I will be more careful about what I say to her. I will feel glad to get some things off my chest but I won't feel helped.

More time will pass.

I will find a better therapist.

I will move on from the relationship.

I will make peace with it all and feel okay.

But right now — I can only notice how sunny it is.

When we get out of the Uber outside of my building, I take note of what a nice day it is for all of this to be over. It is unseasonably warm for early November, and it feels like a celebration of the end of a miserable seven weeks and six days. This type of day would typically make me want to go for a walk. But I would just like to go home and lay down.

Flying South 2021 Editors

Mary Hennessy (Poetry Editor): Mary was a registered nurse most of her adult life. She returned to school late and fell in with a community of generous, word-crazed people. Her poems have appeared in many journals and anthologies. She is a Pushcart nominee. She also serves as Poetry Editor for an online site: *Vietnam War Poetry*. Poetry is the only thing that makes sense to her anymore.

Jennifer Stevenson Vincent (Creative Non-Fiction): Jennifer was twice nominated for the Pulitzer Prize with a speciality in Civil Rights issues. She has a distinguished career in print journalism, including senior staff writer at the St. Petersburg (Fla.) Times. A founder and past President of Winston-Salem Writers, she's taught creative non-fiction at New York University, the University of South Florida and Salem College.

Ray Morrison (Fiction Editor): Ray is an award-winning writer whose stories have appeared in numerous journals and magazines, including *Ecotone, Carve, Beloit Fiction Journal,* and *Fiction Southeast.* He is the author of the story collections, *In a World of Small Truths* (Press 53) and *I Hear the Human Noise* (Press 53). *I Hear the Human Noise* was awarded the 2020 IPPY Gold Medal for Southeast – Best Regional Fiction.

Bob Shar (Fiction Reader): Bob has been writing short stories for over fifty years -- reading and loving them for over sixty. His stories have appeared in *The South Carolina Review, Greensboro Review, Stoneboat, 2 Bridges Review, Bartleby Snopes, Literary Orphans* and elsewhere. He's a former factory worker, journalist, little magazine mogul (founded/edited/nearly-went-broke-running *The Crescent Review*, 1983-87), two-time Pushcart Prize nominee, retired librarian and village idiot.

Steve Lindahl (Fiction Reader): Steve Lindahl is the author of seven novels, *Motherless Soul* (ATTMP), *White Horse Regressions* (ATTMP), *Hopatcong Vision Quest* (Solstice), *Under a Warped Cross* (Solstice), *Living in a Star's Light* (Self Published), *Chasing Margie* (Solstice), and *Woodstock to St. Joseph's* (Solstice). His short fiction has appeared in *The Alaska Quarterly*, *The Wisconsin Review*, *Eclipse* and others. He served for five years on the staff of *The Crescent Review*. (www.stevelindahl.com)

Contributors

Laura Alderson: At ten Laura earned fifty cents a poem—okay, it was from her father, but nonetheless a wildly productive year. It's been bread and overhead through writing ever since. She has been a finalist for the *North Carolina Poetry Society's Poet Laureate Award* twice (first finalist in 2021) and is honored to have made their awards annual five times. Her chapbook and poetry broadside were published by Geryon Press through an NEA grant. She remains grateful to my mentors Carolyn Kizer and Rosanne Coggeshall and indebted to the notorious *Porch Poets* who keep her going.

Genevieve Allaire: Genevieve is a PhD scientist studying plant allelopathy at New Mexico State University. Previous published works of hers have appeared in the *Arak Anthology* and the *Main Street Journal* (Delaware), the *Moab Sun News* (Utah), and *The Fieldstone Review* (Saskatchewan, CA).

Terry Barr: Terry's latest essay collection, *The American Crisis Playlist* (2020-2021), will be published this fall by Redhawk Publications. His essay, "*Greyhound Seats*," won the Spring 2022 *Tell Your Story* nonfiction competition. He writes about music and culture at medium.com/@terrybarr, and lives in Greenville, SC, with his family.

Jenny Bates: She has lived in the Piedmont Foothills for 26 of her 39 years as a resident of North Carolina. She is locally known, in Stokes County, as an animal whisperer especially to Donkeys, Coyotes and "Crow Folk." Her experience is full of friendships she would never have thought possible. Adjacent to Hanging Rock State Park, she has blurred the lines between what is tame and what is not. Her surroundings for the most part are still and peaceful and timeless. The woods go on and on forever, you think, and there's nobody in them but you. Her poetry reflects all of this unique relationship she has to the area of land and the company of animals she keeps. Her poetry yearns and transfigures itself, like nature. Jenny Bates is a member of *Winston-Salem Writers*, *NC Poetry Society*, and *NC Writers Network*. Her published books include, *Opening Doors*: an equilog of poetry about Donkeys (Lulu Publishing, NC 2010); *Coyote with Coffee* (Catbird on the Yadkin Press, NC 2014). *Visitations*, Hermit Feathers Press, NC 2019). *Slip*, (Hermit Feathers Press, NC 2020). Her new collection, *Where the Deer Sleep*, will be published by (Hermit Feathers Press, NC 2022).

Vivian I. Bikulege: Vivian is an emerging North Carolina poet with an MFA in creative non-fiction from Queens University of Charlotte. Recently, she has been awarded the honor of working as the adult emerging poet in western NC in the *Gilbert-Chappell Distinguished Poet* series. In 2022, she was recognized with honorable mentions in the *Randall Jarrell Poetry* competition and *McDill* competition sponsored by the *NC Poetry Society*. She is working to create her first chapbook.

Norma Bourland: Norma is a writer currently living in Minneapolis, MN. enjoying old age with her very old husband and middle-aged Bischon. She is the author of a Kindle book, *Vibrant Old Woman*, and has had articles in *Minnesota Women's Press*, *Christianity Today*, *Chicken Soup for the Soul*. Norma enjoys writing about aging for women in the Gran Finale stage of life on her blog www.vibrantoldwoman.com . Some of Norma's favorite authors include Robert Powers, Anna Quindlan, Anne Lamott, Maya Angelo, and Barbara Brown Taylor. When she is not writing, Norma enjoys collage and fabric art, her 5 grandchildren and community volunteer work.

Katie Bowers: Katie is a poet and educator living in the rural Southeast with her husband and daughter. Her work has been recently published in *Qu Literary Magazine*, *Haunted Waters Press*, and *The Dewdrop*, for which she was nominated for The Pushcart Prize.

Noah Brown: Noah just recently graduated from Florida State University with a Bachelor's in Creative Writing. He mainly writes poetry, specifically narrative free verse.

Matt Cheek: Matt served in the Marine Corps from 2006 - 2011 and deployed to Iraq, Afghanistan, and Africa as a Cryptologic Linguist and earned the rank of Sergeant. He later graduated from UNC Chapel Hill and the USC Marshall School of Business. Matt currently works in risk management at KPMG and lives in Charlotte, NC with his wife, son, and dog. His first written work, Lucas, earned third place in Charlotte Lit's LIT/South Awards for Nonfiction. Matt encourages all readers to donate to the Camaraderie Foundation in order to help further the organization's goal of healing the invisible wounds of war.

Kathie Collins: Kathie Collins, Cofounder & Creative Director of *Charlotte Center for Literary Arts*, is a poet, mythologist, and lifelong student of Jungian psychology—which, consciously and unconsciously, makes its way into her work. She earned her graduate degrees in Mythological Studies at Pacifica Graduate Institute, where she also served as adjunct faculty. Kathie thrives in the in-between spaces from which dreams and creativity emerge, and she's happiest when she can share those spaces, bringing words and people together for transformative conversations. Kathie is author of *Jubilee* (Main Street Rag). Her poems have appeared in *Immanence, Kakalak, Pedestal Magazine*, and elsewhere.

Bill Colvard: Bill is a former journalist, reporter for the Mount Airy News, and editor of the Elkin Tribune, where he was a four-time 1st-place award winner with the *North Carolina Press Association* for column writing.

Mary Ann Crowe: Mary Ann lives in Santa Fe, New Mexico. Her poems have been published or are forthcoming in *Sin Fronteras /Writers Without Borders, Miriam's Well,* and *Trickster Literary Journal.* "*War Child Lament 2020*" was a poetry prize winner for the *Pasatiempo*

Writing Contest. As a visual artist-activist-writer, her essays, art installations and public art projects have addressed gender, the environment, war and gun violence. Barnard College graduate born in Munich, Santa Fe is her 30th move between Germany, New York, Chicago, and Puerto Rico.

Andrew DeVoy: Andrew is from the desert of Southern California. He has an interdisciplinary BA in Linguistics and English, an old dog, and a wonderful partner who fills their house with plants and fresh bread while they figure out their twenties together. He currently works from home for a tech company in the Pacific Northwest but he would like to teach someday. His poetry has been published in *Burning Jade Magazine*.

N. G. Haiduck: N. G. is pleased to be among the writers to appear in *Flying South 2022*. She is the recipient of the *Jerome Lowell DeJur Award in Creative writing* from The City College of New York, *the BRIO (Bronx Recognizes Its Own) Award* from the Bronx Council on the Arts, and the *Janice Farrell Poetry Prize* from the National League of American Pen Women. Publications include *Prairie Home Companion, Hanging Loose, Paterson Literary Review, InterPoezia,* and *New York City Streets in Poetry.* She thanks her husband, clarinetist Neal Haiduck, for his help in writing this profile of Sonny Truitt.

John Haugh: John's writing has been published in *The North Carolina Literary Review, Notre Dame Magazine, Main Street Rag, Rat's Ass Review, The Wall Street Journal, The Tipton Poetry Journal, storySouth* and elsewhere. He won the *2022 Randall Jarrell Poetry Prize*, which left him giddy, was selected for *Poetry in Plain Sight,* and a few other things. Haugh lives in North Carolina, was a good fencer once and spends untold hours in bookstores like Scuppernong and Bookmarks. When not helping fix that supply chain problem, he works on his next book.

Jo Ann Hoffman: Jo Ann's publications include the non-fiction narrative, *Angels Wear Black,* short fiction and poetry in literary journals, including *Persimmon Tree, New Verse News, Broad River Review, Red Clay Review, Kakalak* and *Flying South* among others. She is a Pushcart nominee and has received contest awards from the *North Carolina Poetry Society* and the *Palm Beach Poetry Festival.*

Sharon Louise Howard: Sharon holds BA and MA degrees from the University of Central Florida, with concentrations on literature and writing. She is a Pushcart nominee. Her poetry and fiction have appeared in *Flying South, Cricket, Streetlight Magazine, Orange Blossom Review, Literally Stories*, among others.

Earl Carlton Huband: Earl (Durham, NC), is the author of *The Innocence of Education* (Longleaf Press, 2018) and *In the Coral Reef of the Market* (Main Street Rag Publishing, 2020). The latter won the *2021 Peace Corps Writers Best Book of Poetry Award.*

Emma Jahoda-Brown: Emma is a writer and photographer. She holds a BFA in photography and media from California Institute of the Arts and an MFA in poetry from Columbia University. She splits her time between New York City and Los Angeles.

Gordon Lindsey: Gordon, raised as a nomadic army brat, has engaged in three writing careers. For 30 years he specialized in corporate communications, including house organs and executive speeches. Upon retiring, he entered into the Presbyterian ministry, writing weekly sermons. He also authors a blog that draws an international readership. Now retired again, he is reclaiming his orphan, poetry writing. He and his wife live in Charlottesville, Virginia.

Amy Marques: Amy grew up between languages and cultures and learned, from an early age, the multiplicity of narratives. She penned three children's books, barely read medical papers, and numerous letters before turning to short fiction. Her work has been published or is forthcoming in anthologies and journals including *Star82 Review, Jellyfish Review, MoonPark Review, Flying South, Streetcake:*

Experimental Writing Magazine, and *Sky Island Journal.* You can find her at @amybookwhisper1 or read more of her words at https://amybookwhisperer.wordpress.com.

Evelyn Menary: Evelyn is a Canadian writer who loves to become immersed in the writing process, to the point of being inside the story. All that is needed then is to look around, listen and to record the world that unfolds there.

Emma Grace Myers: Emma is a writer based in New York City. She was raised in upstate New York and attended SUNY Purchase, graduating summa cum laude with a BA in Playwriting/Screenwriting in 2018. emmagracemyers.com

Greg Nelson: Greg Nelson is a former teacher and a depression survivor. He received an M.F.A. in poetry from George Mason University. His wilderness adventures include a solo hike through the Grand Canyon. He lives near the Nansemond River in Suffolk, VA. Recent publications include poems in *Snapdragon, Penultimate Peanut, BEATIFIC Magazine* and *Gyroscope Review.* His work is forthcoming in *Atlanta Review.*

Leslie Parker: Leslie has received recognition for her work as a finalist in the Bucks County (PA) Poet Laureate Competition in 1993, again, as a runner-up in 1995, and has won multiple awards from *The Poetry Council of North Carolina* and *The North Carolina Poetry Society.* Her poetry has appeared in several literary journals including *Bay Leaves, Black Buzzard Review, The Cape Rock, Cold Mountain Review, Half Tones to Jubilee, Hawaii Review, Medical Literary Messenger, The Panhandler* and numerous others. In addition, one of her poems appeared on posters throughout North Carolina in February 2022 as part of the *NC Poetry Society's Poetry in Plain Sight* program. She lives in McLeansville, North Carolina.

Barbara Rizza Mellin (cover artist): Barbara is a painter/printmaker from Winston-Salem, NC. As an art historian, she loves reinterpreting traditional techniques and methods for contemporary audiences. The cover image is a white-line linocut, printed by hand using non-toxic inks. The white-line technique was first introduce in the early 20th century by a group of women known as The Provincetown Printmakers, who wanted to produce multicolor prints using one block. Mellin's art has appeared in juried exhibitions throughout the US, in galleries, universities and museums and internationally online. www.BarbaraRizzaMellin.com

David E. Poston: David is the author of two award-winning poetry chapbooks and the full-length collection *Slow of Study*. His poetry, fiction, and reviews have appeared in *Pembroke Magazine*, *Reedy Branch Review*, *North Carolina Literary Review*, *Pedestal Magazine*, and many other journals and anthologies. He is a co-editor of *Kakalak*.

Anya Russian: Anya (Greensboro, NC) is currently completing a master's degree in peace and conflict studies. In both her research and in life she likes to work across disciplines: as a dance-artist, avid rock climber, literary translator, language educator, and editor. Her poems have been featured in *International Poetry Review*, *Pinesong* (Poet Laureate Award, 2010), and two editions of the *Nazim Hikmet Poetry Festival Anthology*. She is happy to be back in North Carolina after surviving several Canadian winters in grad school.

Joyce Schmid: Joyce's work recently appeared or is forthcoming in *Hudson Review*, *Five Points*, *Literary Imagination*, and other journals and anthologies. She lives with her husband of over half a century in Palo Alto, California.

Cynthia Singerman: Cynthia, a Florida native, is a writer living in San Francisco. She holds a bachelor's degree in English literature and Spanish, as well as a law degree from the University of Florida. Her work has appeared or is forthcoming in *Sky Island Journal*, *Dillydoun Review*, *Sou'wester Literary Journal*, *HerStry*, *Streetlight Magazine*, *Menda City Review*, *Litbreak Magazine*, *American Writers Review*, and

COG Magazine. She is currently working on her novel, set in San Francisco.

Hunt Smith: Hunt is currently an Algebra 1 teacher in Nashville, Tennessee; however, he majored in English at Sewanee. *Day Drinking* is his first publication.

Mark Smith-Soto: Costa Rican-American, Mark, has authored four prize-winning chapbooks and three full-length poetry collections, *Our Lives Are Rivers* (University Press of Florida, 2003), *Any Second Now* (Main Street Rag Publishing Co., 2006) and *Time Pieces* (Main Street Rag Publishing Co., 2015). His work has appeared in *The Bitter Oleander, Kenyon Review, Literary Review, Nimrod, Poetry East, Rattle, The Sun* and many other publications and been nominated several times for a Pushcart Prize. In 2006 it was recognized with an NEA Fellowship in Creative Writing. His book of translations *Fever Season: Selected Poetry of Ana Istarú* (2010) and his lyrical memoir *Berkeley Prelude* (2013) were both published by Unicorn Press.

Quentin Steadman: Quentin is a third-year MFA student at Old Dominion University in Norfolk, VA. His undergraduate English degree was earned at Middle Tennessee State University of Murfreesboro, TN. He was born and raised in Franklin, Kentucky - where the only notable thing about the town is being the setting for the marriage between June Carter and Johnny Cash (not that they had much choice - only Kentucky allowed couples to obtain a marriage certificate and tie the knot on the same day). When he is not reading or writing he is trying his best to put one foot in front of the other and take each day as it comes. He enjoys music as much as writing, his original intended degree in undergrad being Audio Production; music in some capacity will typically grace the stage of any story of his.

Nick T. Watson: Nick, originally from Buenos Aires, now lives in South Carolina. He is currently at work on his first collection of short stories, some of which have reached the final rounds of *Carve Magazine*, *Gival Press*, *Cutbank* and *Glimmer Train* contests.

Lillo Way: Lillo's poetry collection, *Lend Me Your Wings*, was released in July 2021 by Shanti Arts Publishing. Her chapbook, *Dubious Moon*, won the *Slapering Hol Press Chapbook Contest*. Her poems have won the *E.E. Cummings Award* and a *Florida Review Editors' Prize*. Her writing has appeared in such journals as *New Letters*, *Poet Lore*, *Tampa Review*, *Poetry East*, and in many anthologies. Way has received grants from the NEA, NY State Council on the Arts, and the Geraldine R. Dodge Foundation for her choreographic work involving poetry. www.lilloway.com.

Kevin Winchester: Kevin lives in Waxhaw, North Carolina and holds an MFA in Creative Writing from Queens University. His debut novel, *Sunflower Dog*, was released in spring of 2020 by *SFK Press*. His story, *"Waiting on Something to Happen,"* won the *2013 Thomas Wolfe Fiction Prize* and he was named Charlotte's (NC) 2021 Favorite Writer in Charlotte Magazine's annual *Best of the Best Awards*. *Main Street Rag* published his short story collection, *Everybody's Gotta Eat* in 2009. His writing has appeared in *Tin House*, *Gulf Coast*, *StorySouth*, *Barrelhouse*, *Dead Mule* and the anthologies *Everything But the Baby* and *Making Notes: Music of the Carolinas*, among others. When he's not writing, teaching, or hanging with his family, he's either hiking or playing music.